STONE ARCH BOOKS

a capstone imprint

STONE ARCH BOOKS™
Published in 2013
A Capstone Imprint
1710 Roe Crest Drive
North Mankato, MN 56003
www.capstonepub.com

Originally published by DC Comics in the U.S. in
single magazine form as Tiny Titans #8.

DC Comics
1700 Broadway, New York, NY 10019
A Warner Bros. Entertainment Company

Cataloging-in-Publication Data is available at the Library of Congress website:
ISBN: 978-1-4342-4699-8 (library binding)

Summary: School's in session at Sidekick City Elementary, and it's time for report cards! Plus, even more heroics and hilarity from the Tiny Titans!

STONE ARCH BOOKS
Ashley C. Andersen Zantop *Publisher*
Michael Dahl *Editorial Director*
Donald Lemke & Alison Deering *Editors*
Heather Kindseth *Creative Director*
Hilary Wacholz *Designer*
Kathy McColley *Production Specialist*

DC COMICS
Jann Jones *Original U.S. Editor*
Stephanie Buscema *U.S. Assistant Editor*

Printed in China by Nordica.
1213/CA21302219
112013 007892R

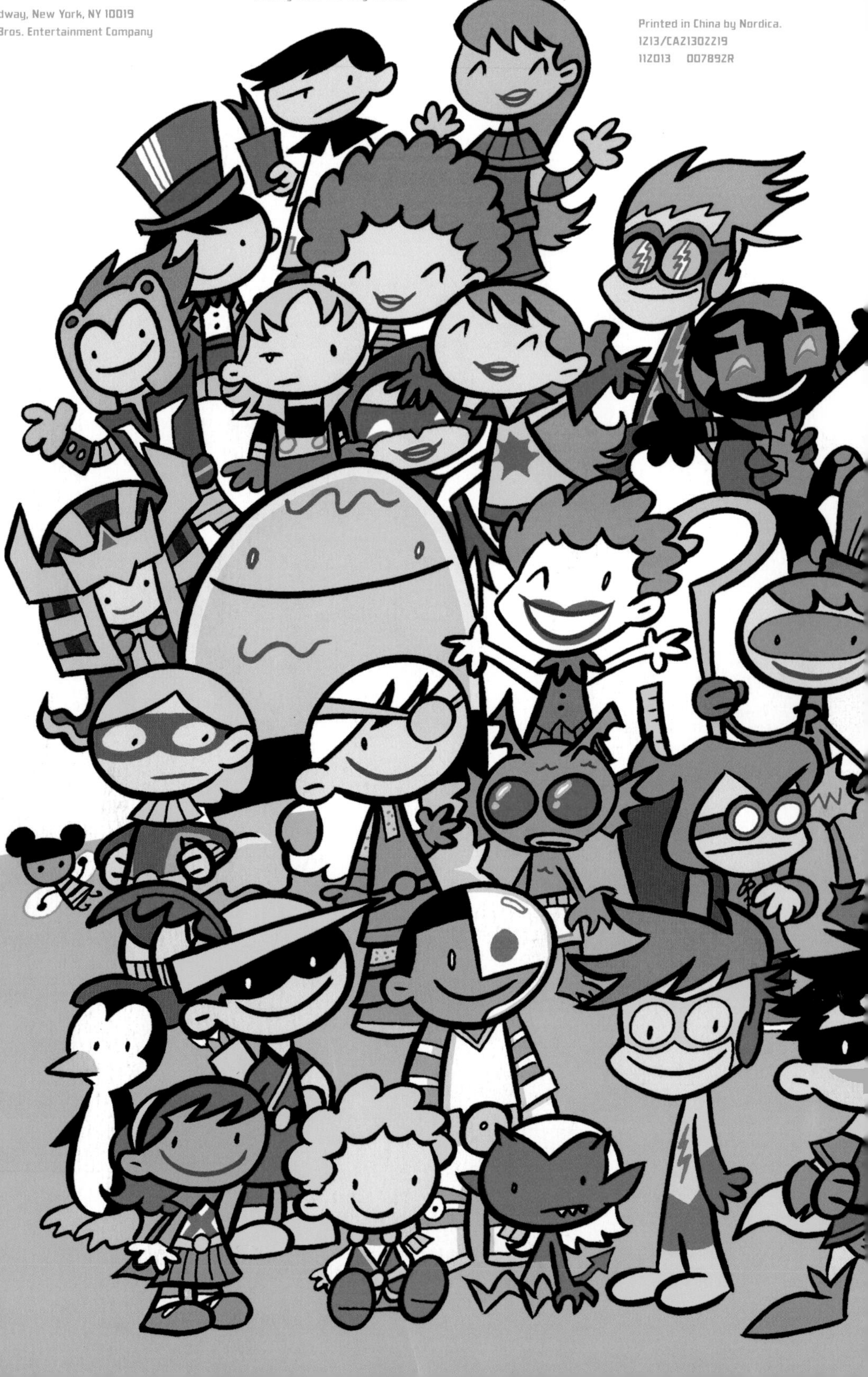

iny titans

Report Card Pickup!

By Eisner Winners
Art Baltazar & Franco

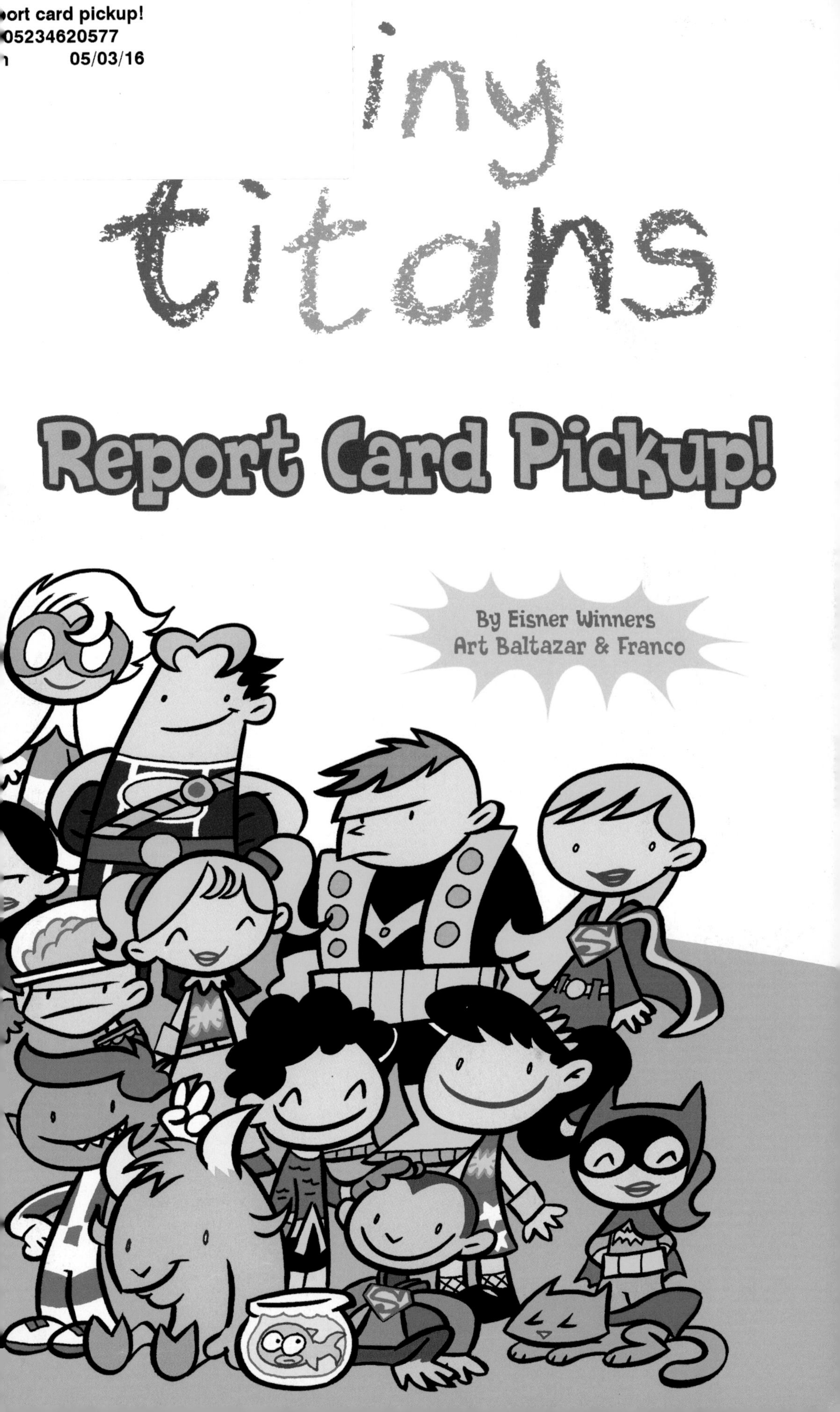

tiny titans

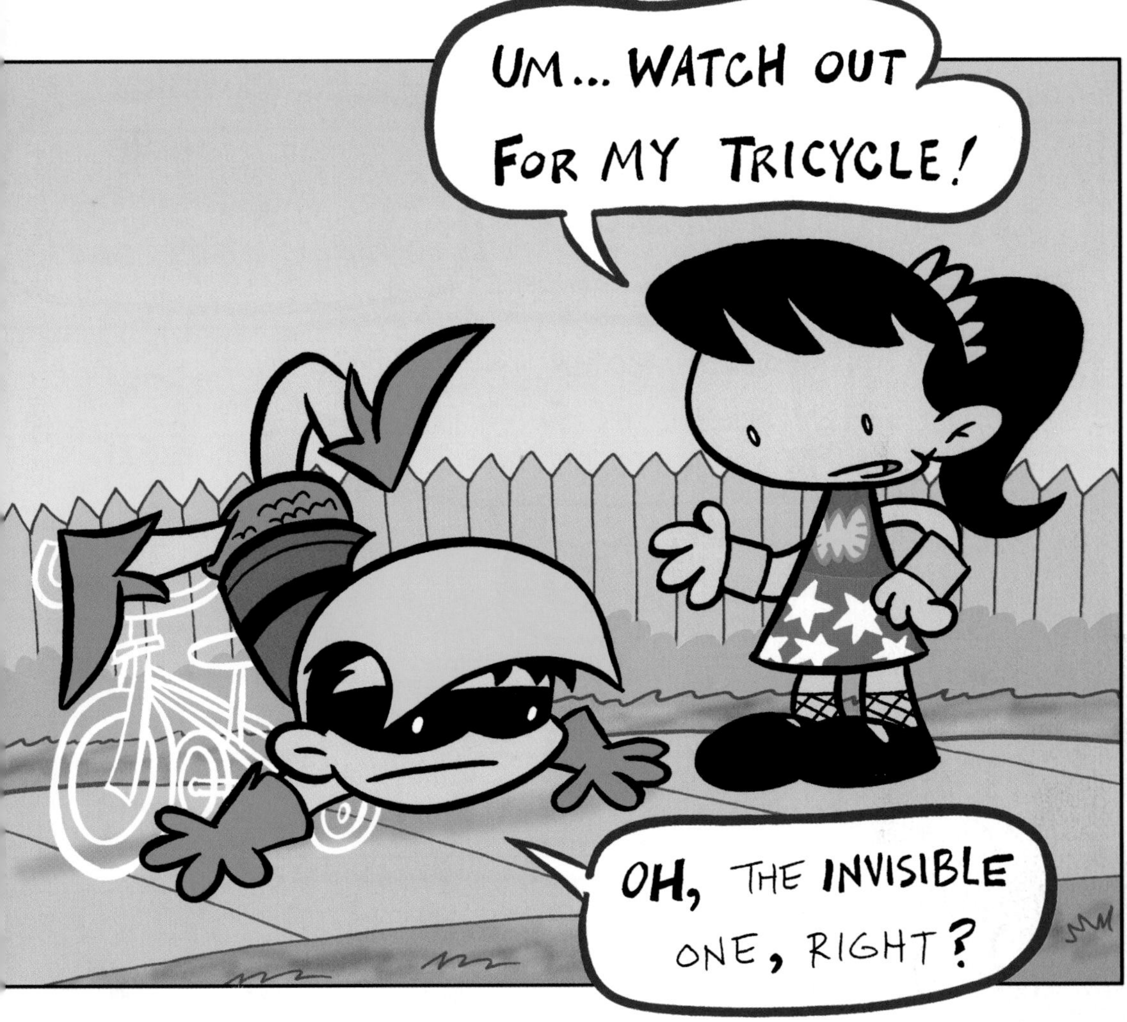
UM... WATCH OUT FOR MY TRICYCLE!
OH, THE INVISIBLE ONE, RIGHT?

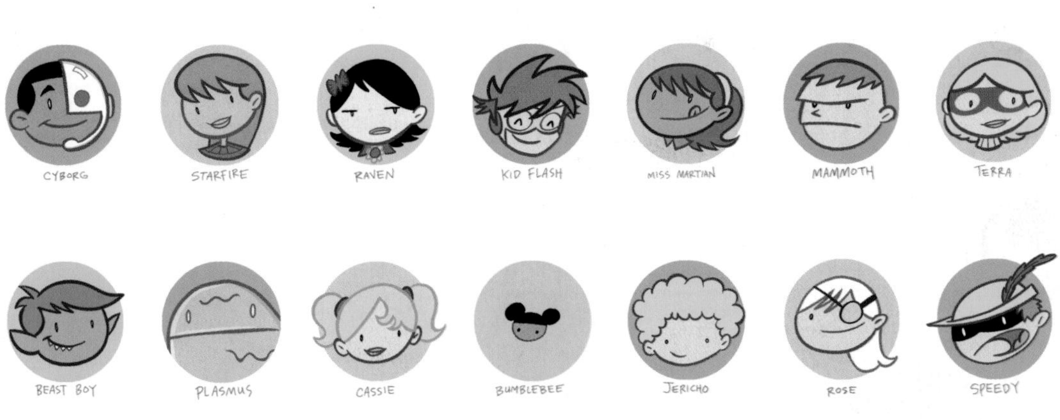
CYBORG
STARFIRE
RAVEN
KID FLASH
MISS MARTIAN
MAMMOTH
TERRA
BEAST BOY
PLASMUS
CASSIE
BUMBLEBEE
JERICHO
ROSE
SPEEDY

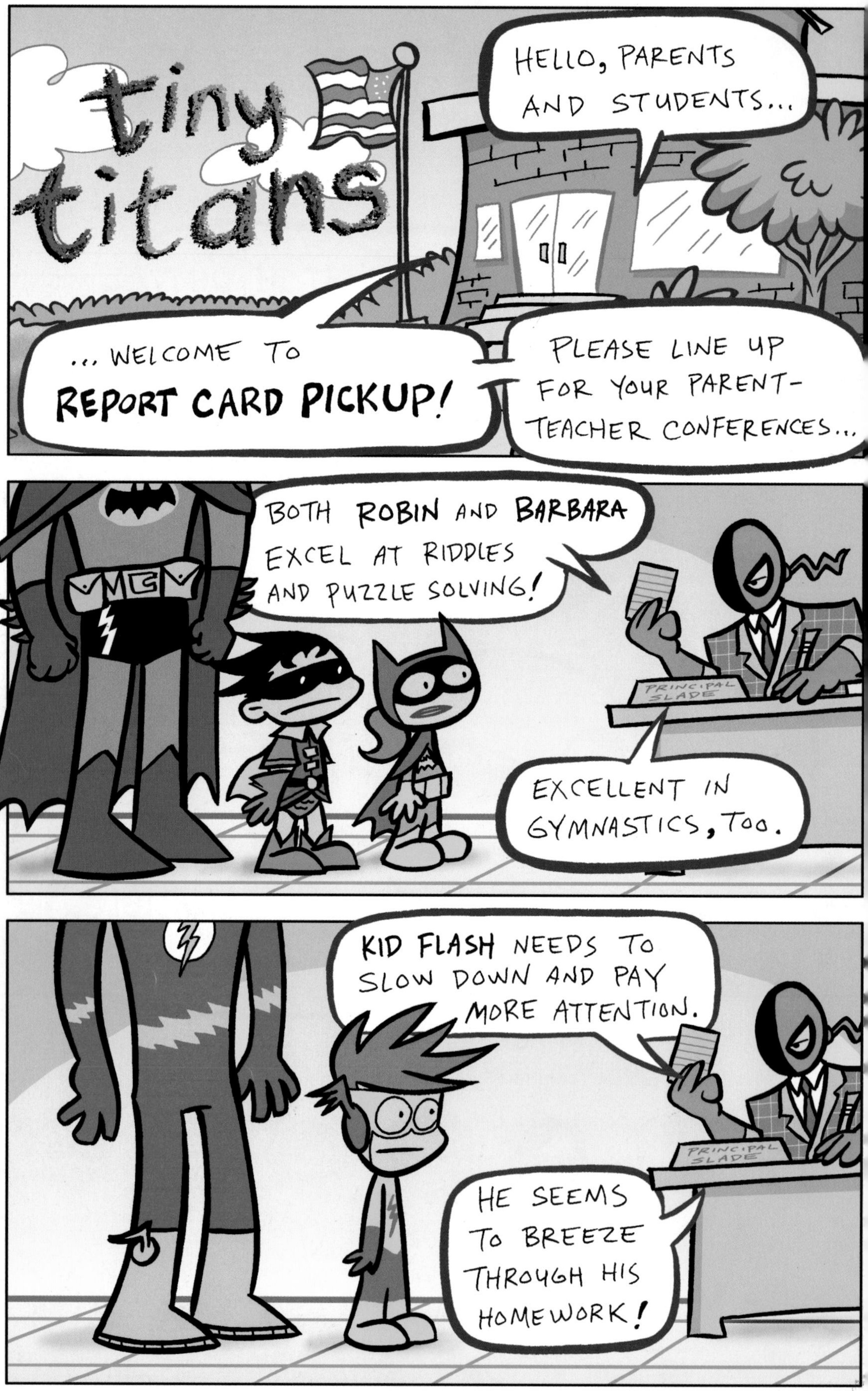

tiny titans
HELLO, PARENTS AND STUDENTS...
... WELCOME TO REPORT CARD PICKUP!
PLEASE LINE UP FOR YOUR PARENT-TEACHER CONFERENCES...
BOTH ROBIN AND BARBARA EXCEL AT RIDDLES AND PUZZLE SOLVING!
PRINCIPAL SLADE
EXCELLENT IN GYMNASTICS, TOO.
KID FLASH NEEDS TO SLOW DOWN AND PAY MORE ATTENTION.
PRINCIPAL SLADE
HE SEEMS TO BREEZE THROUGH HIS HOMEWORK!

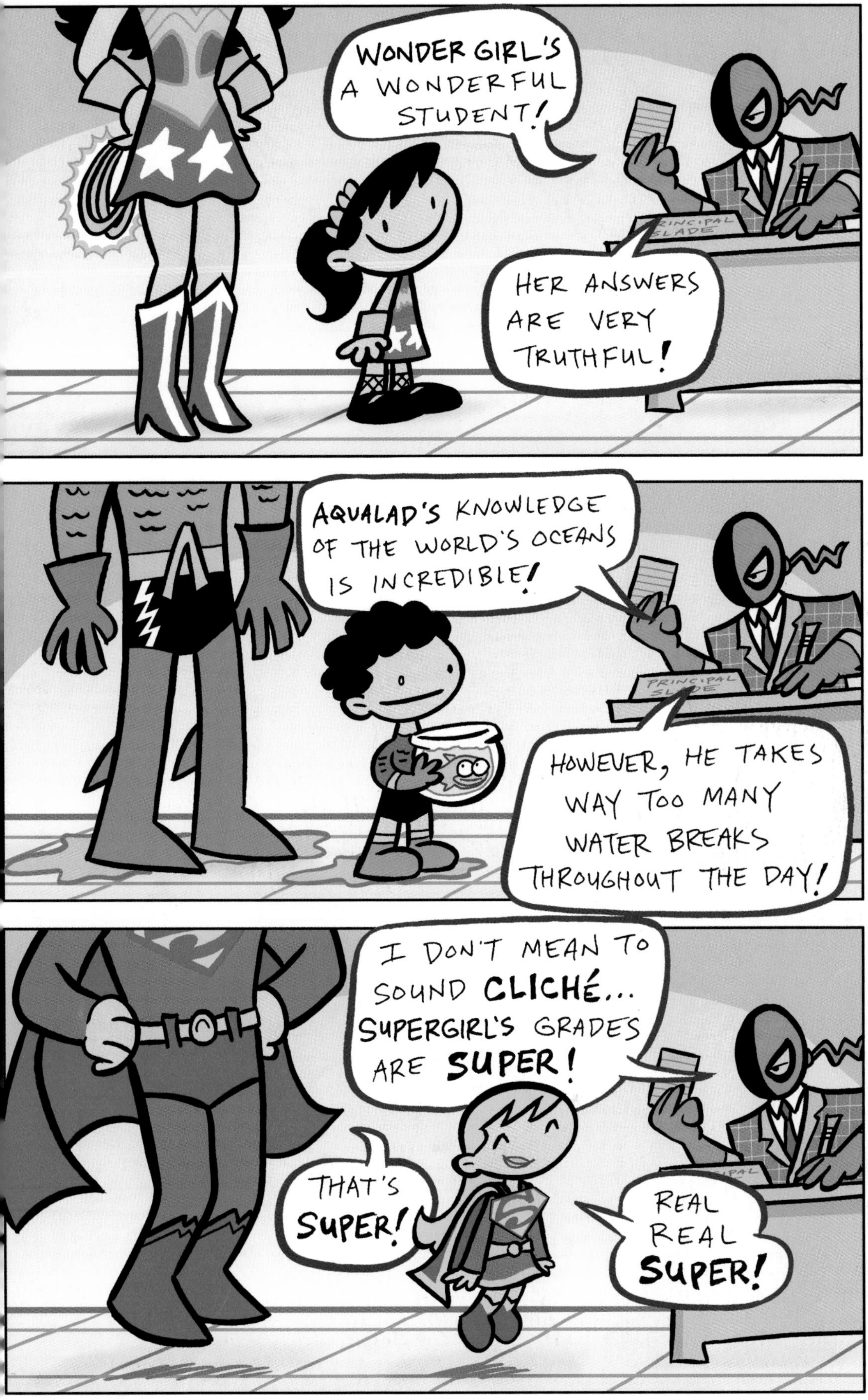
WONDER GIRL'S A WONDERFUL STUDENT!
HER ANSWERS ARE VERY TRUTHFUL!
PRINCIPAL SLADE
AQUALAD'S KNOWLEDGE OF THE WORLD'S OCEANS IS INCREDIBLE!
PRINCIPAL SLADE
HOWEVER, HE TAKES WAY TOO MANY WATER BREAKS THROUGHOUT THE DAY!
I DON'T MEAN TO SOUND CLICHÉ... SUPERGIRL'S GRADES ARE SUPER!
THAT'S SUPER!
REAL REAL SUPER!

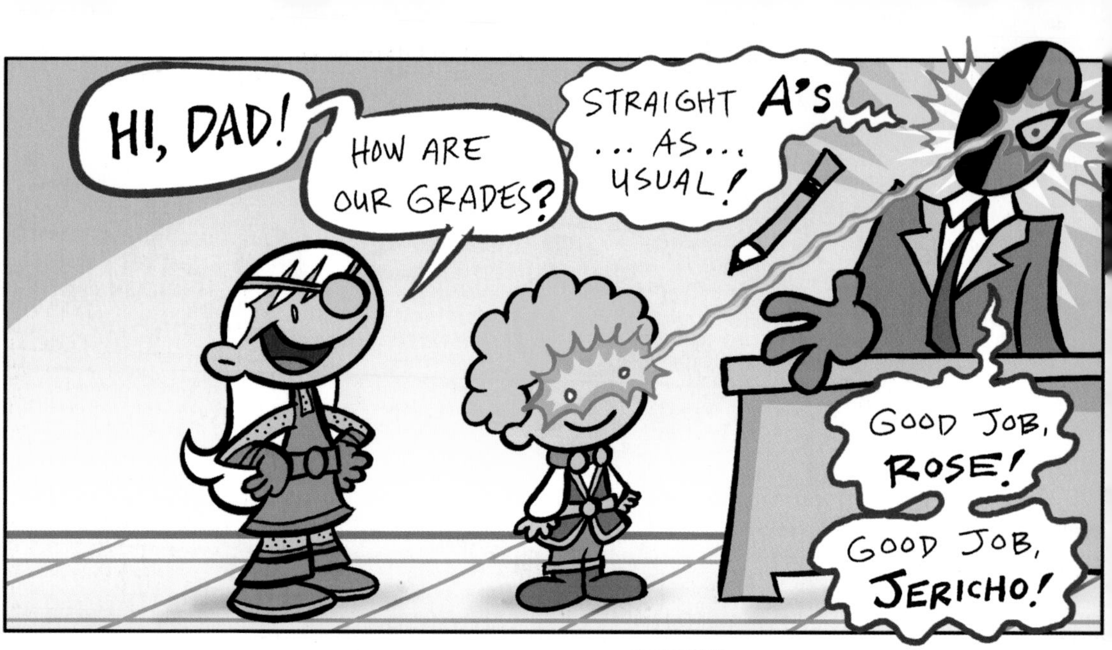
HI, DAD!
HOW ARE OUR GRADES?
STRAIGHT A'S ... AS... USUAL!
GOOD JOB, ROSE!
GOOD JOB, JERICHO!

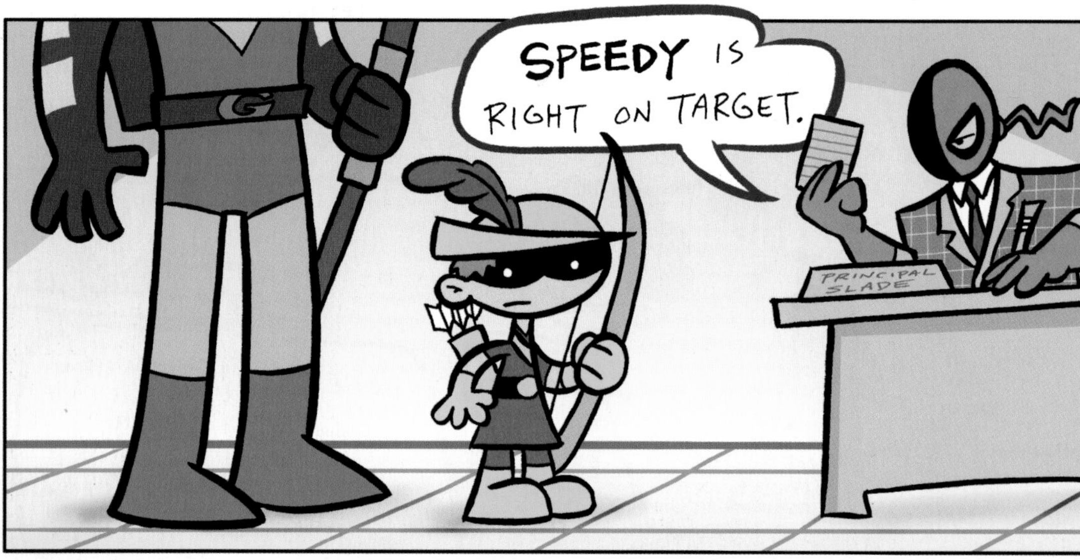
SPEEDY IS RIGHT ON TARGET.
PRINCIPAL SLADE

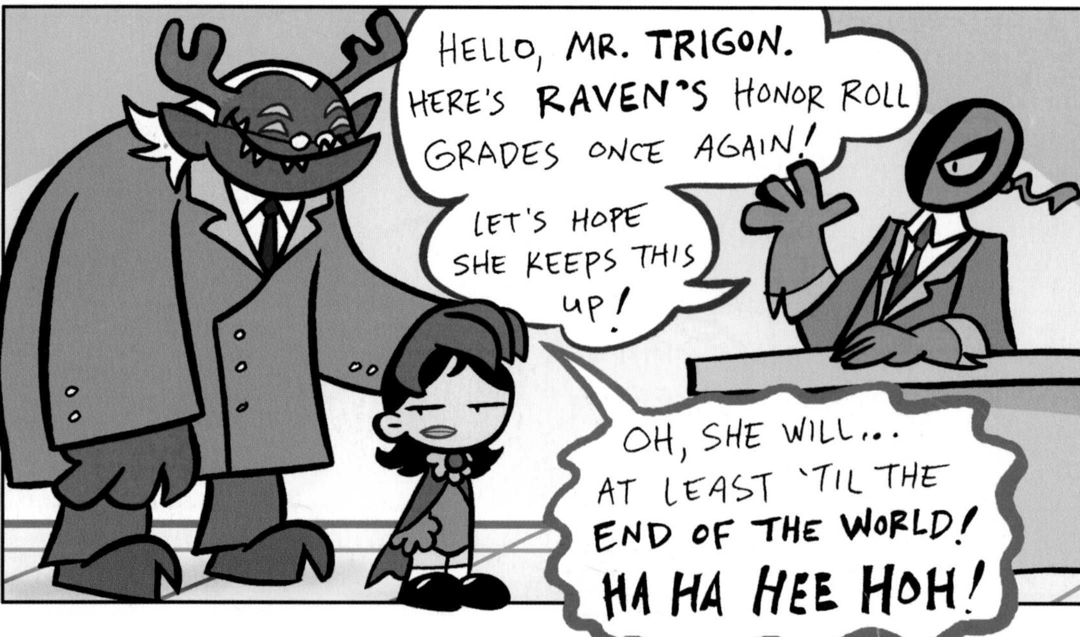
HELLO, MR. TRIGON. HERE'S RAVEN'S HONOR ROLL GRADES ONCE AGAIN!
LET'S HOPE SHE KEEPS THIS UP!
OH, SHE WILL... AT LEAST 'TIL THE END OF THE WORLD! HA HA HEE HOH!

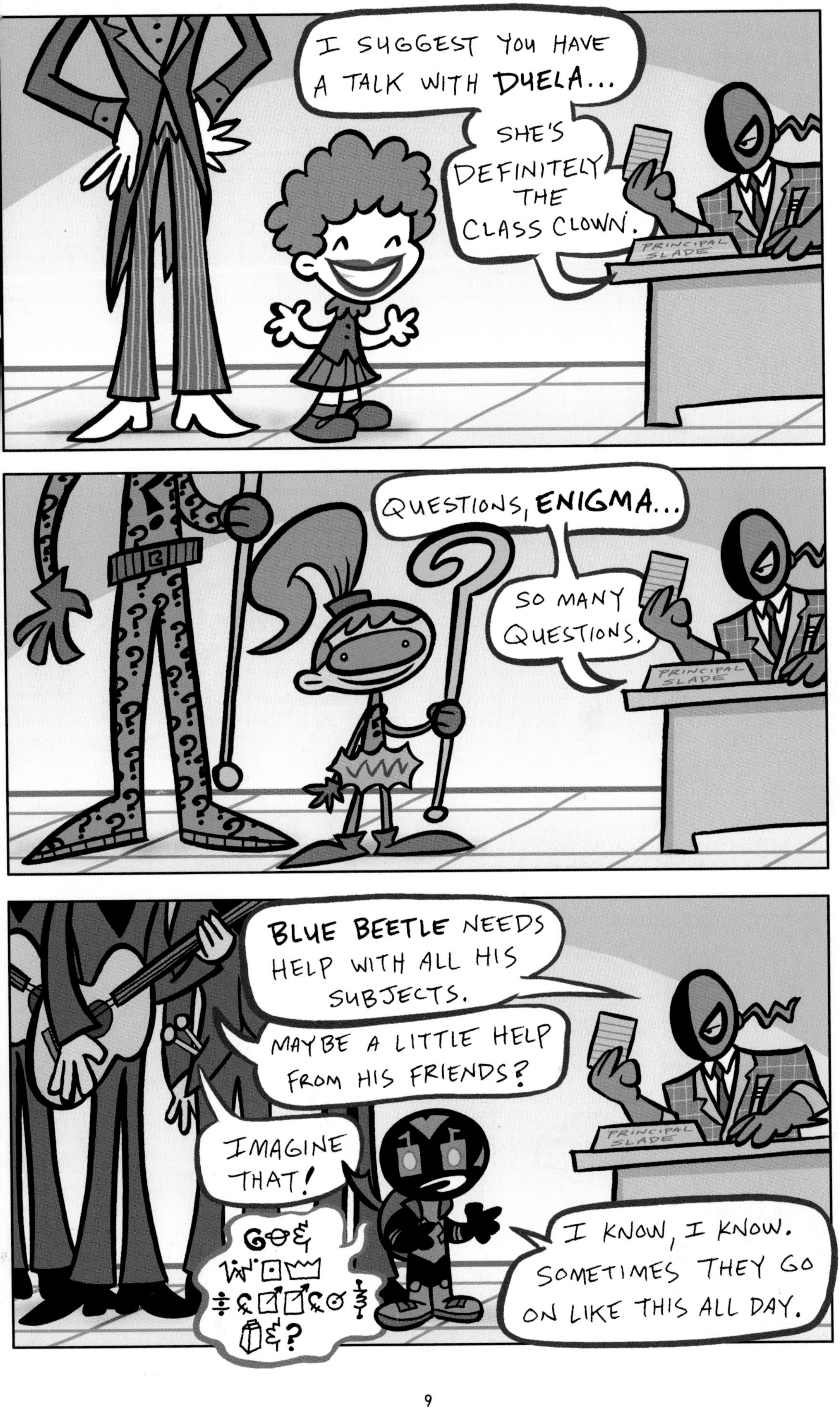
I SUGGEST YOU HAVE A TALK WITH DUELA...
SHE'S DEFINITELY THE CLASS CLOWN.
PRINCIPAL SLADE
QUESTIONS, ENIGMA...
SO MANY QUESTIONS.
PRINCIPAL SLADE
BLUE BEETLE NEEDS HELP WITH ALL HIS SUBJECTS.
MAYBE A LITTLE HELP FROM HIS FRIENDS?
PRINCIPAL SLADE
IMAGINE THAT!
I KNOW, I KNOW. SOMETIMES THEY GO ON LIKE THIS ALL DAY.

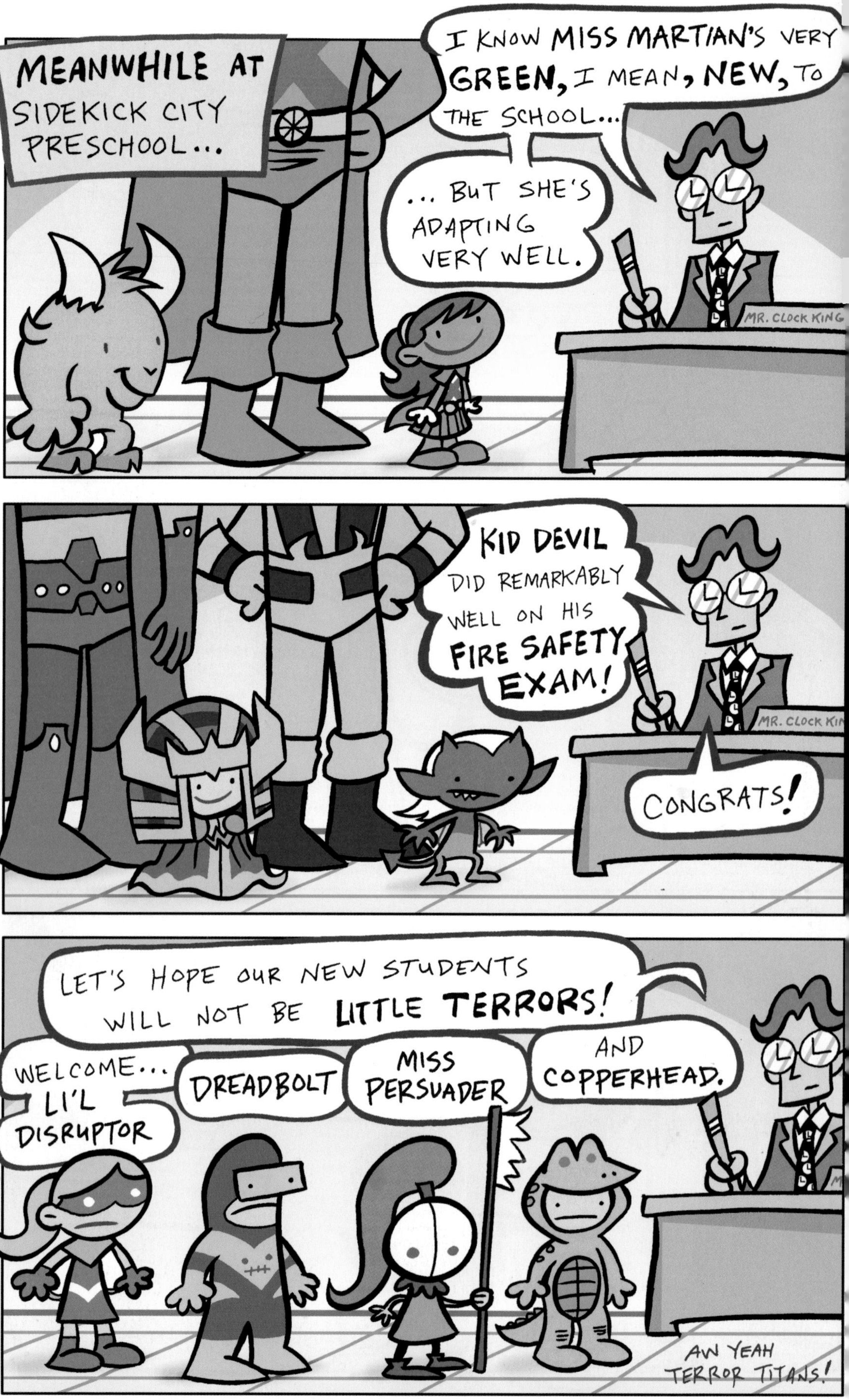

MEANWHILE AT SIDEKICK CITY PRESCHOOL...
I KNOW MISS MARTIAN'S VERY GREEN, I MEAN, NEW, TO THE SCHOOL...
... BUT SHE'S ADAPTING VERY WELL.
MR. CLOCK KING
KID DEVIL DID REMARKABLY WELL ON HIS FIRE SAFETY EXAM!
CONGRATS!
LET'S HOPE OUR NEW STUDENTS WILL NOT BE LITTLE TERRORS!
WELCOME... LI'L DISRUPTOR
DREADBOLT
MISS PERSUADER
AND COPPERHEAD.
AW YEAH TERROR TITANS!

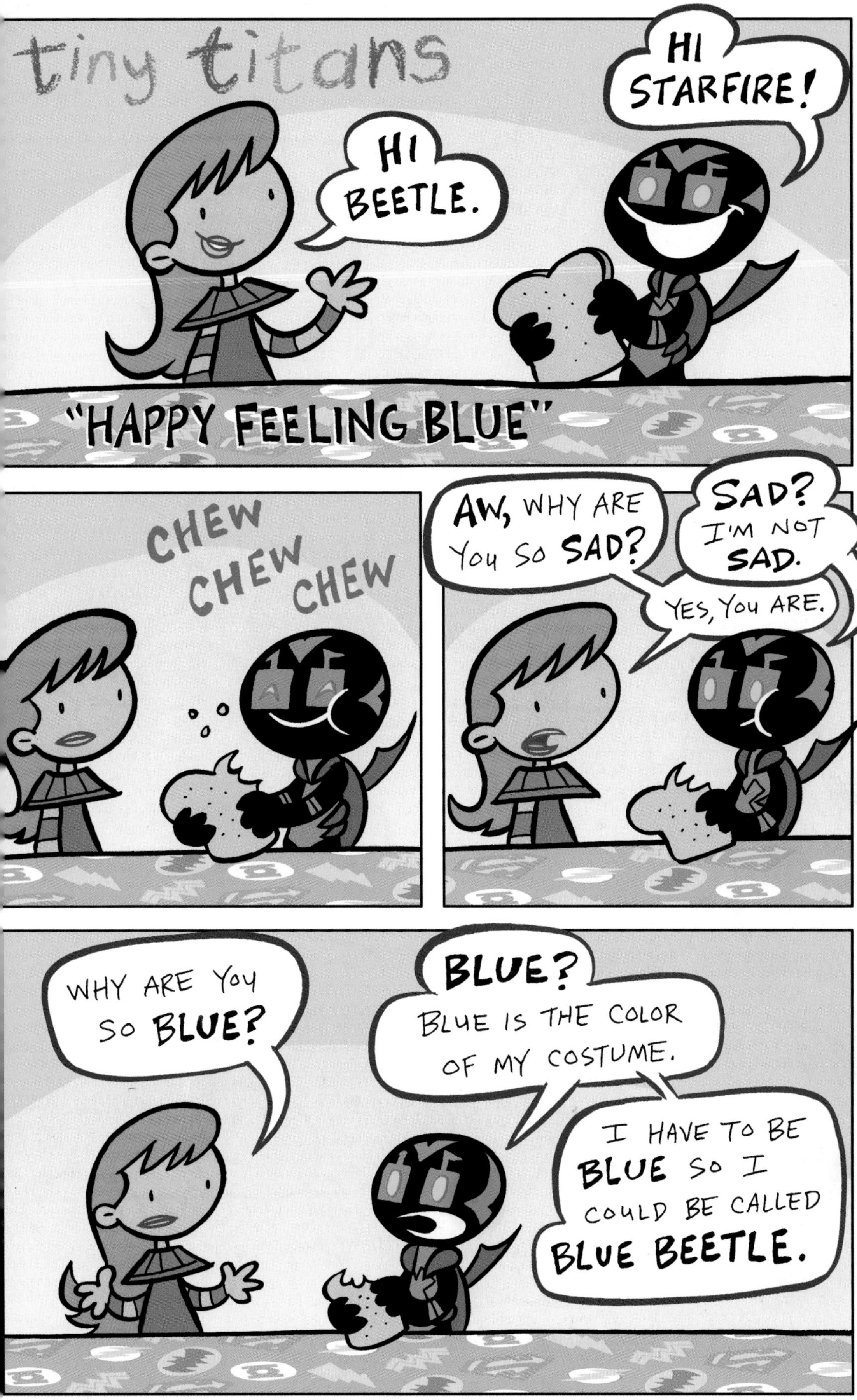
tiny titans
HI STARFIRE!
HI BEETLE.
"HAPPY FEELING BLUE"
CHEW CHEW CHEW
AW, WHY ARE YOU SO SAD?
SAD? I'M NOT SAD.
YES, YOU ARE.
WHY ARE YOU SO BLUE?
BLUE? BLUE IS THE COLOR OF MY COSTUME.
I HAVE TO BE BLUE SO I COULD BE CALLED BLUE BEETLE.

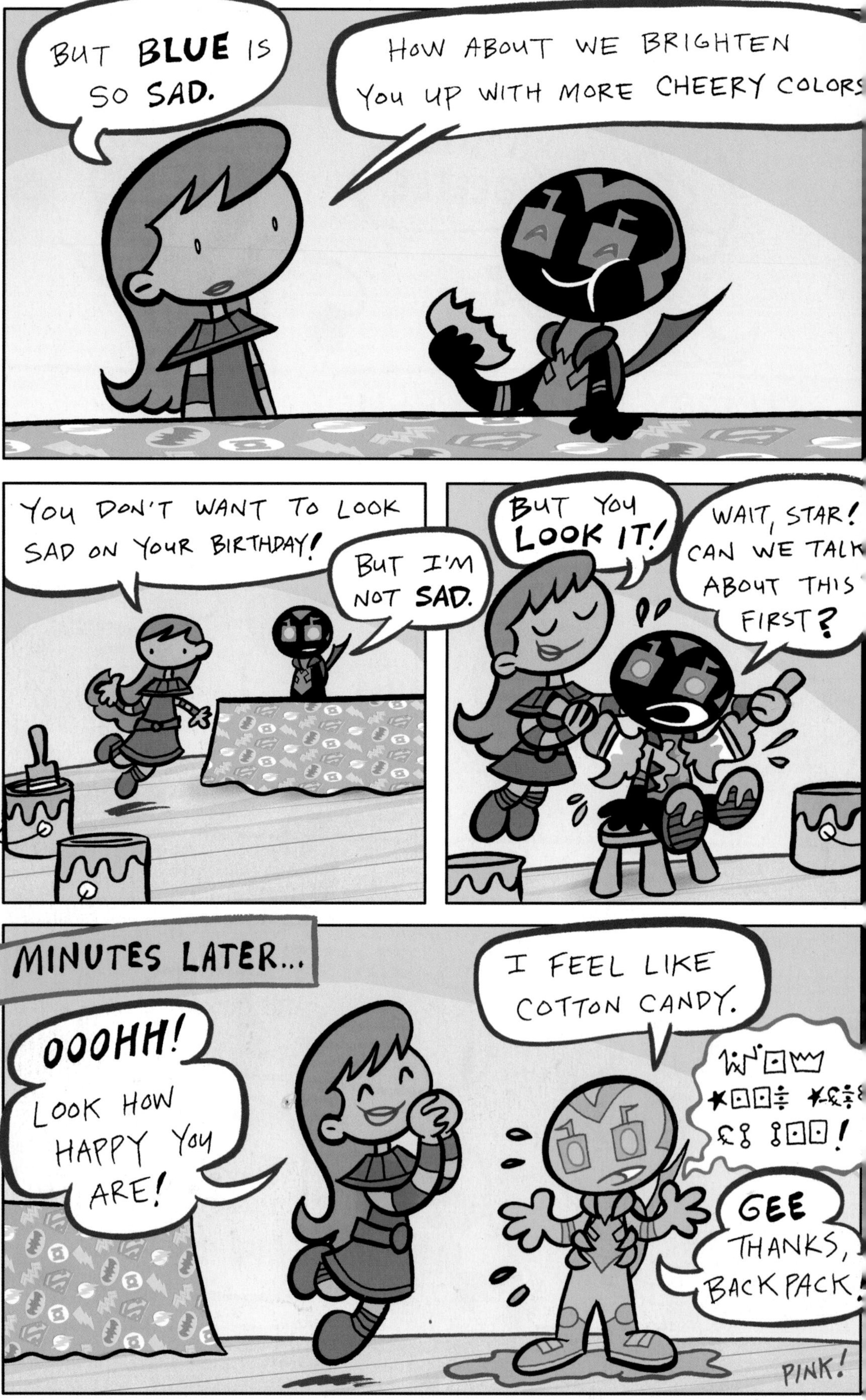

BUT BLUE IS SO SAD.
HOW ABOUT WE BRIGHTEN YOU UP WITH MORE CHEERY COLORS
YOU DON'T WANT TO LOOK SAD ON YOUR BIRTHDAY!
BUT I'M NOT SAD.
BUT YOU LOOK IT!
WAIT, STAR! CAN WE TALK ABOUT THIS FIRST?
MINUTES LATER...
OOOHH! LOOK HOW HAPPY YOU ARE!
I FEEL LIKE COTTON CANDY.
GEE THANKS, BACKPACK!
PINK!

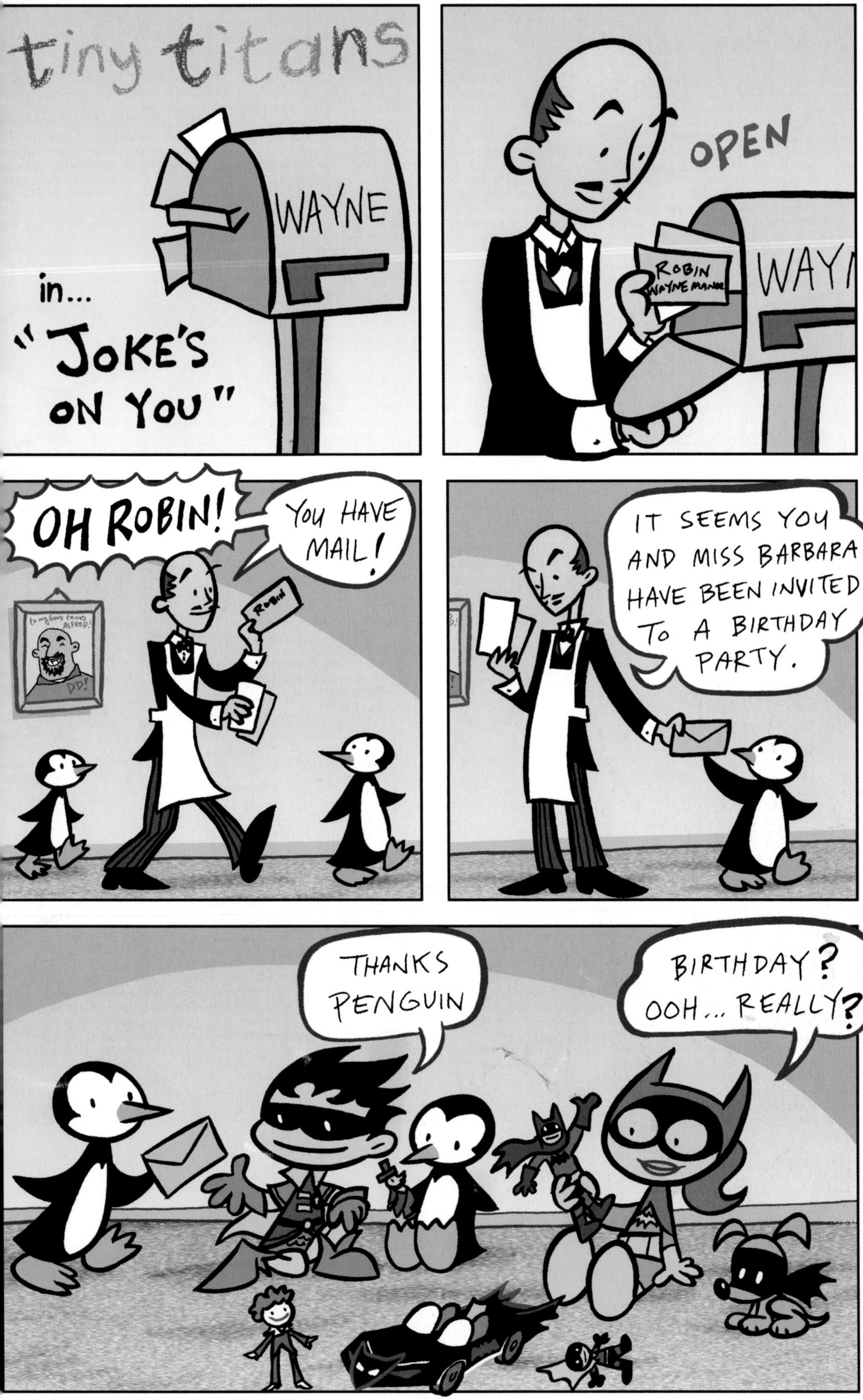
tiny titans
WAYNE
in...
"JOKE'S ON YOU"
OPEN
ROBIN WAYNE MANOR
WAYN
OH ROBIN!
YOU HAVE MAIL!
ROBIN
to my GOOD FRIEND ALFRED!
DD!
IT SEEMS YOU AND MISS BARBARA HAVE BEEN INVITED TO A BIRTHDAY PARTY.
THANKS PENGUIN
BIRTHDAY? OOH... REALLY?

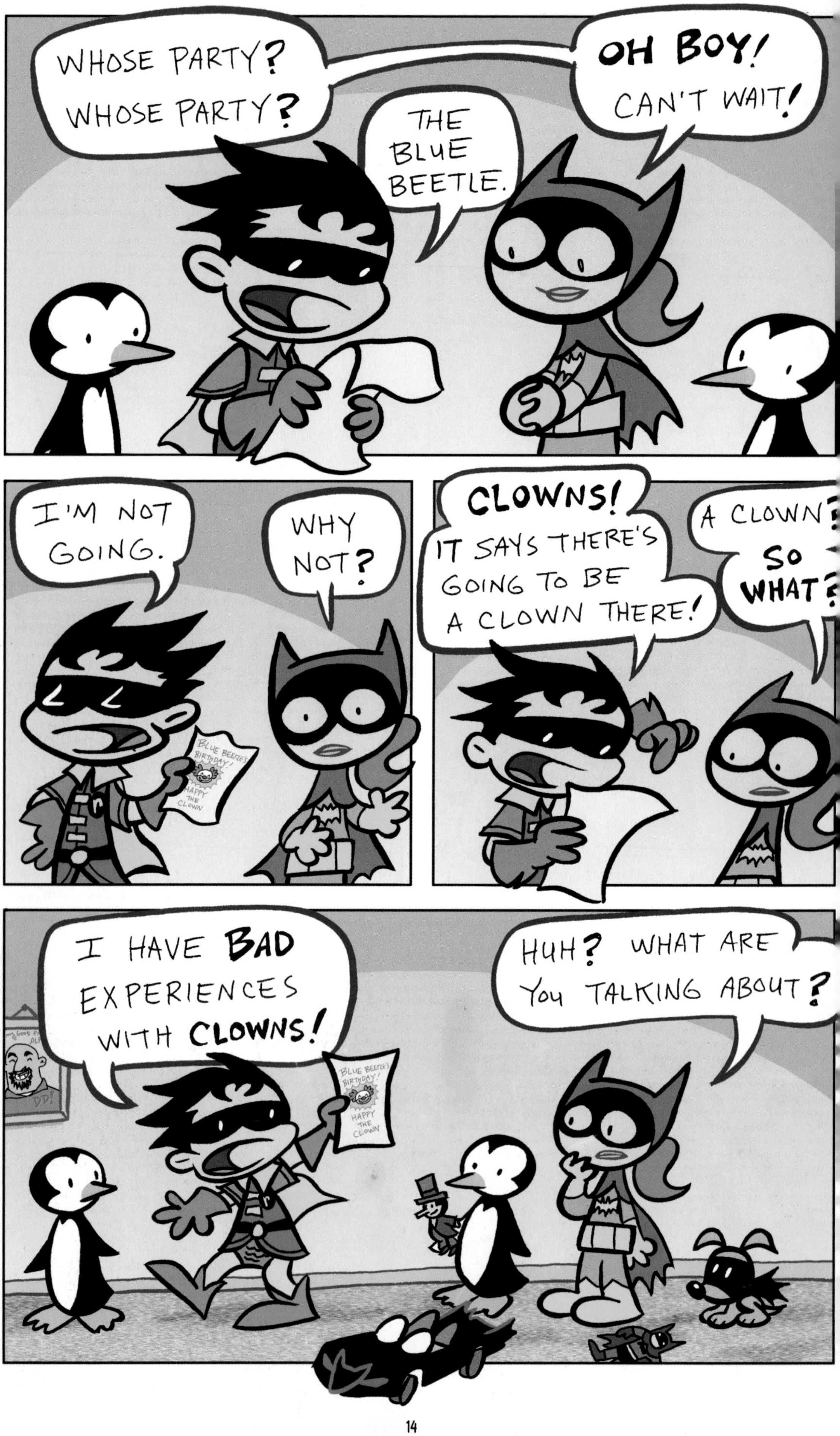
WHOSE PARTY? WHOSE PARTY?
THE BLUE BEETLE.
OH BOY! CAN'T WAIT!
I'M NOT GOING.
WHY NOT?
BLUE BEETLE'S BIRTHDAY! HAPPY THE CLOWN
CLOWNS! IT SAYS THERE'S GOING TO BE A CLOWN THERE!
A CLOWN
SO WHAT
I HAVE BAD EXPERIENCES WITH CLOWNS!
HUH? WHAT ARE YOU TALKING ABOUT?

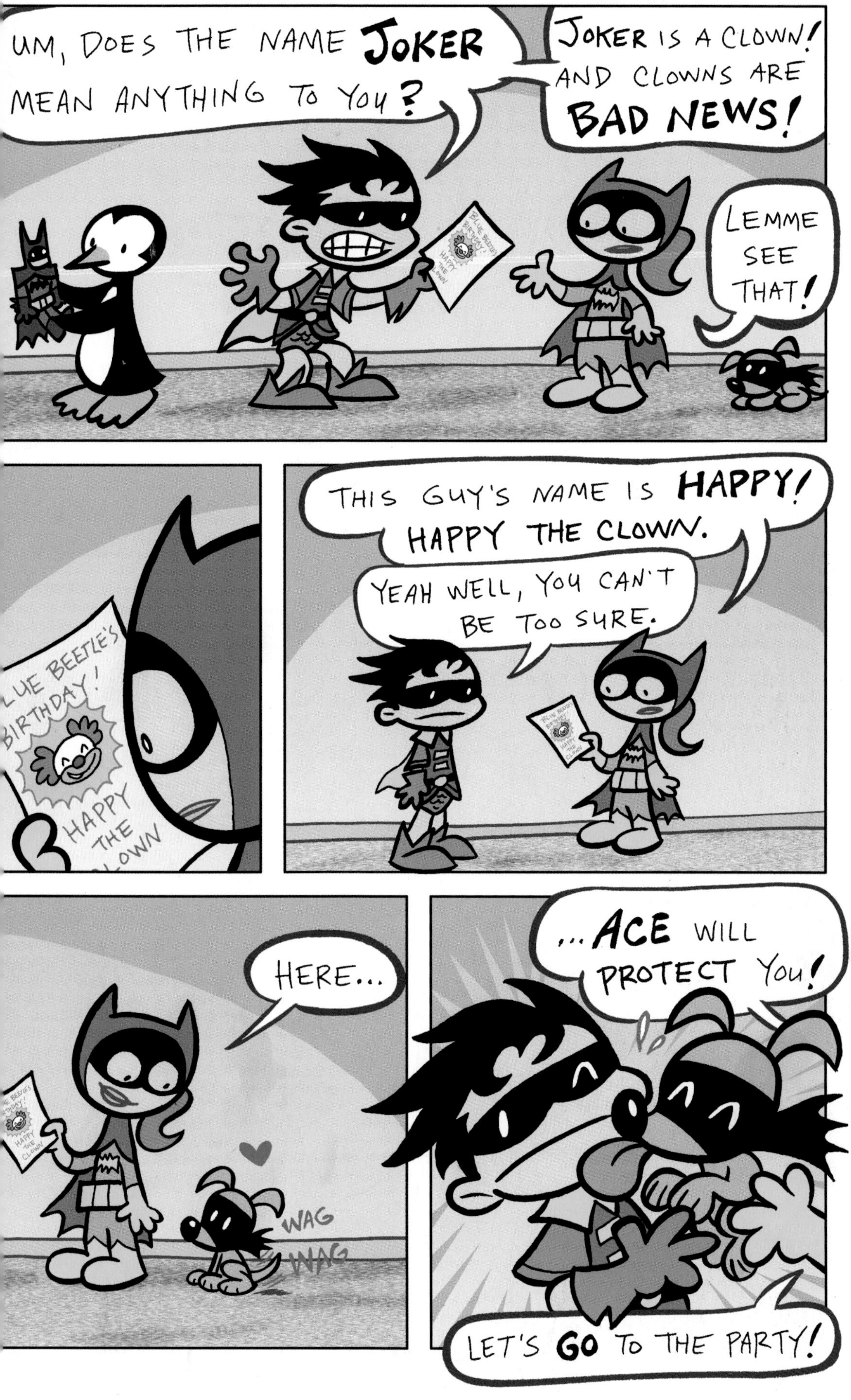
UM, DOES THE NAME JOKER MEAN ANYTHING TO YOU?
JOKER IS A CLOWN! AND CLOWNS ARE BAD NEWS!
BLUE BEETLE'S BIRTHDAY! HAPPY THE CLOWN
LEMME SEE THAT!
LUE BEETLE'S BIRTHDAY! HAPPY THE LOWN
THIS GUY'S NAME IS HAPPY! HAPPY THE CLOWN.
YEAH WELL, YOU CAN'T BE TOO SURE.
HERE...
WAG WAG
...ACE WILL PROTECT YOU!
LET'S GO TO THE PARTY!

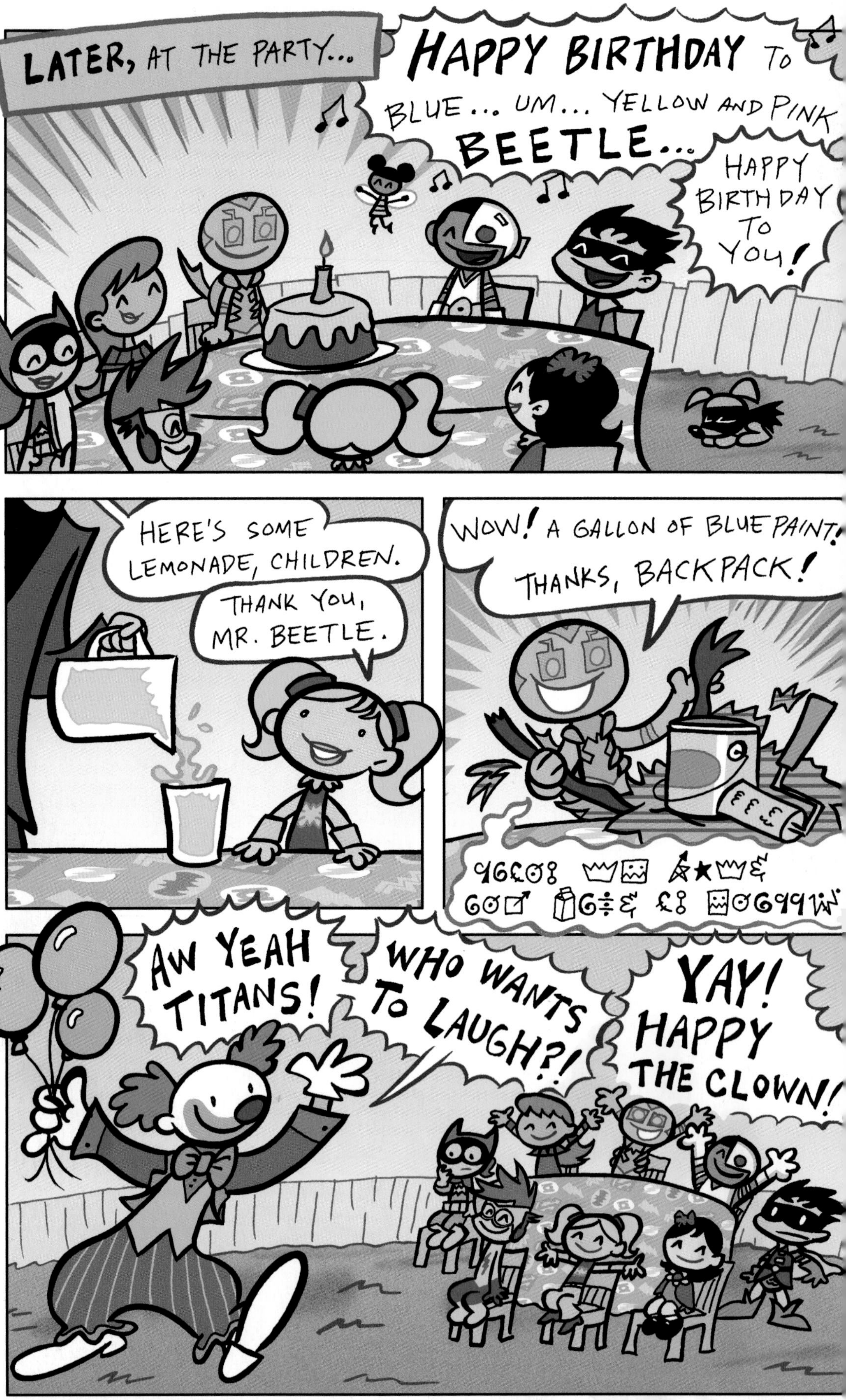
LATER, AT THE PARTY...
HAPPY BIRTHDAY TO BLUE... UM... YELLOW AND PINK BEETLE...
HAPPY BIRTHDAY TO YOU!
HERE'S SOME LEMONADE, CHILDREN.
THANK YOU, MR. BEETLE.
WOW! A GALLON OF BLUE PAINT! THANKS, BACKPACK!
AW YEAH TITANS!
WHO WANTS TO LAUGH?!
YAY! HAPPY THE CLOWN!

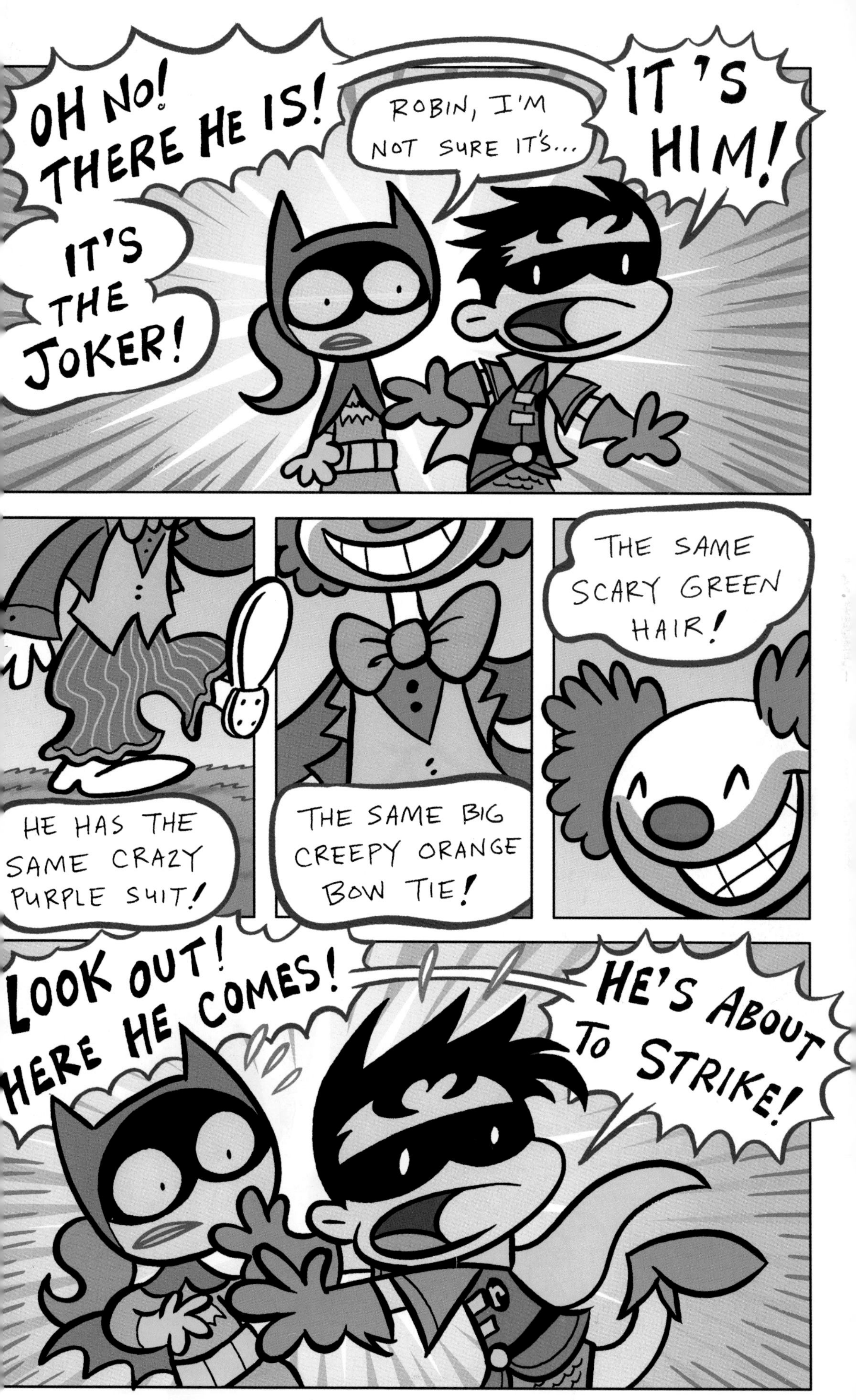
OH NO! THERE HE IS!
IT'S THE JOKER!
ROBIN, I'M NOT SURE IT'S...
IT'S HIM!
HE HAS THE SAME CRAZY PURPLE SUIT!
THE SAME BIG CREEPY ORANGE BOW TIE!
THE SAME SCARY GREEN HAIR!
LOOK OUT! HERE HE COMES!
HE'S ABOUT TO STRIKE!

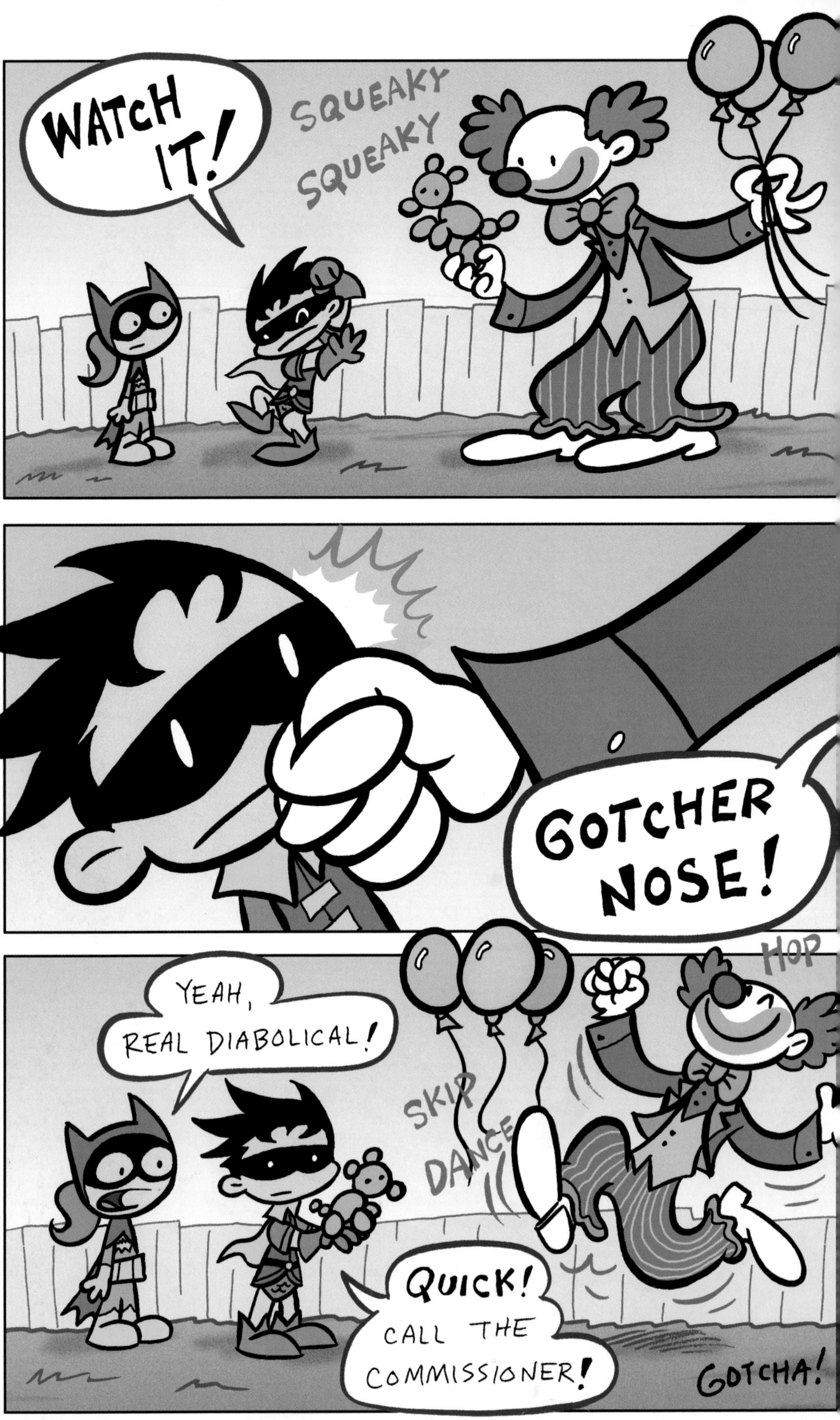
WATCH IT!
SQUEAKY SQUEAKY
GOTCHER NOSE!
YEAH, REAL DIABOLICAL!
HOP
SKIP
DANCE
QUICK! CALL THE COMMISSIONER!
GOTCHA!

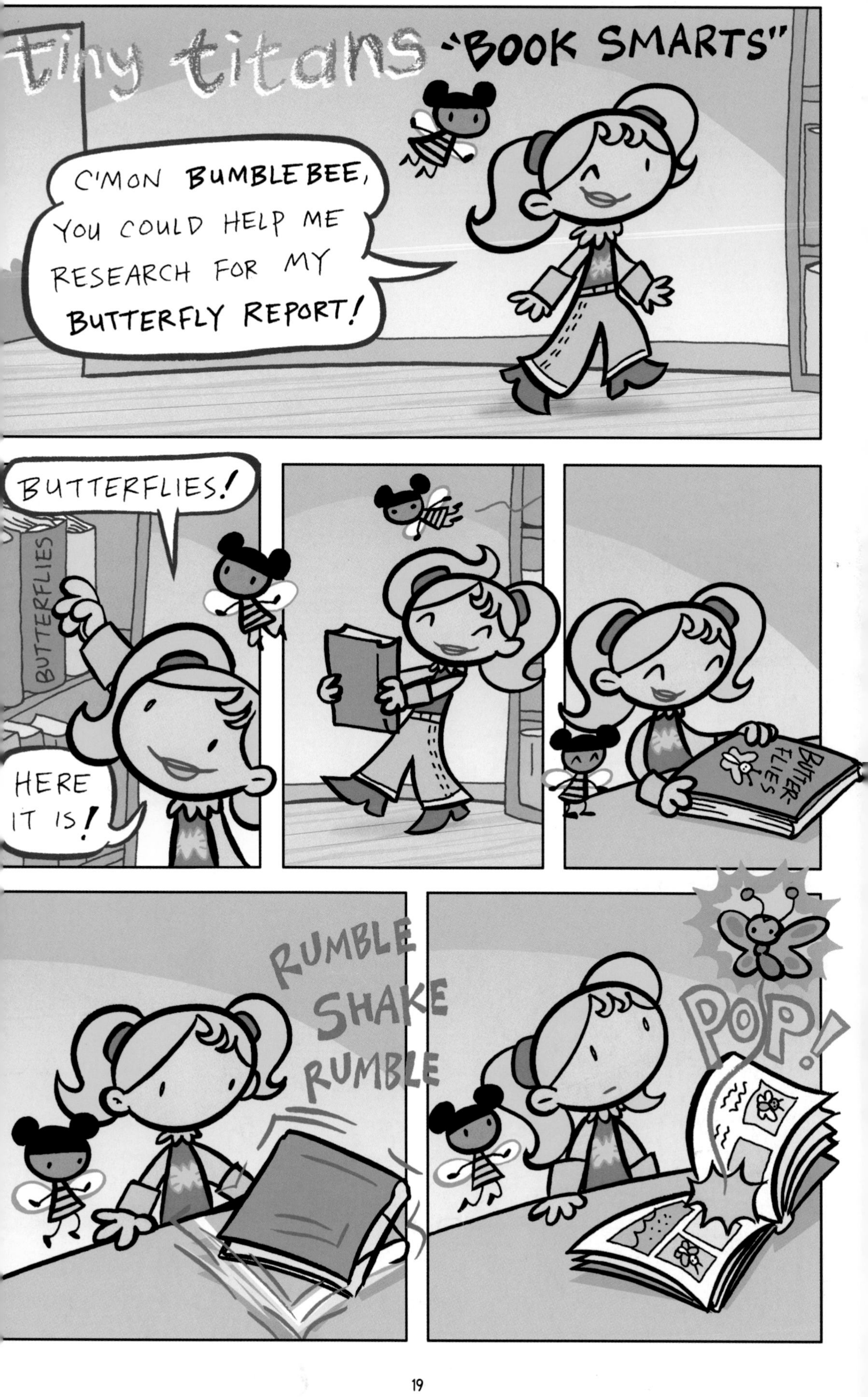
tiny titans
"BOOK SMARTS"
C'MON BUMBLEBEE, YOU COULD HELP ME RESEARCH FOR MY BUTTERFLY REPORT!
BUTTERFLIES!
BUTTERFLIES
HERE IT IS!
BUTTER-FLIES
RUMBLE SHAKE RUMBLE
POP!

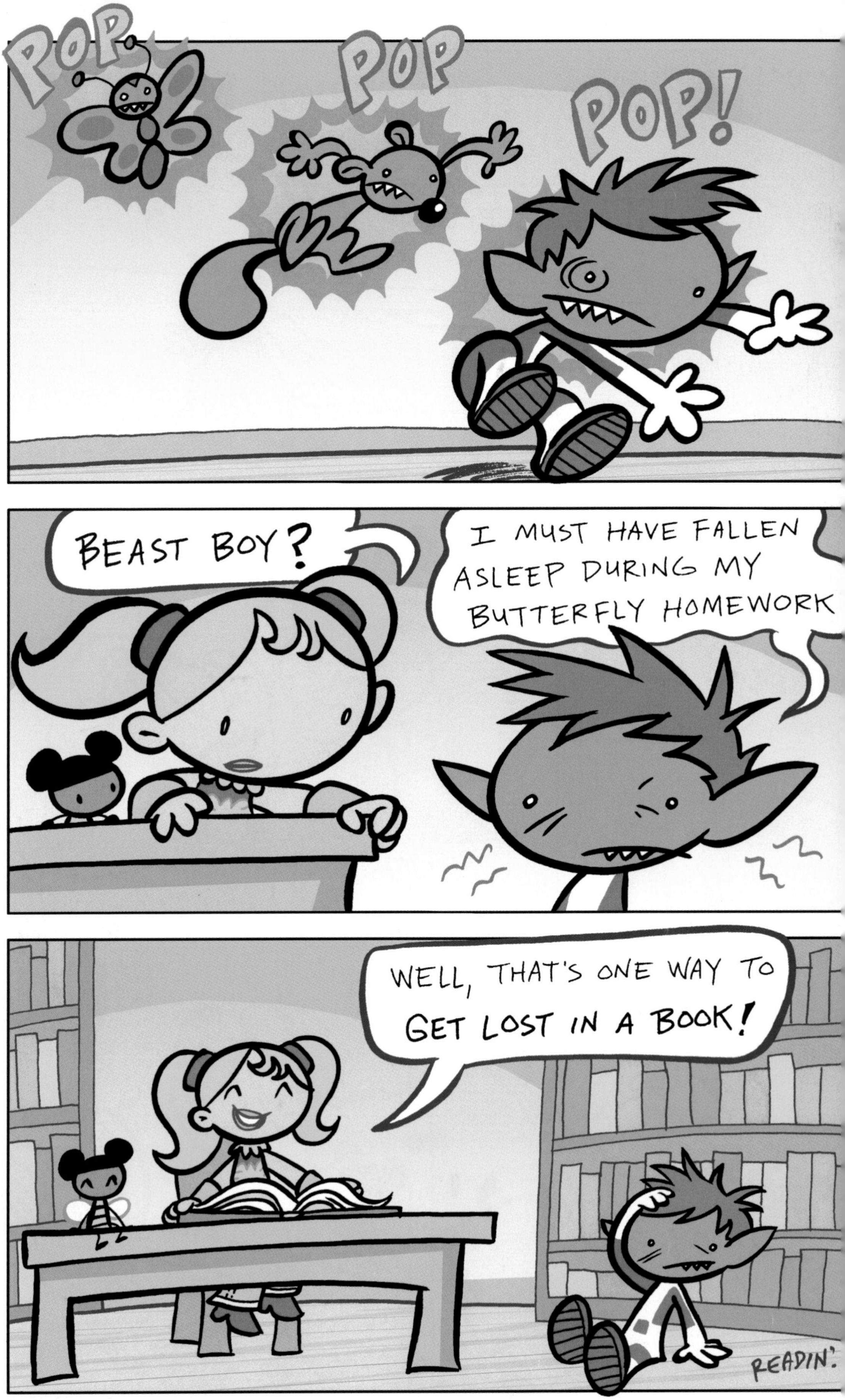
POP
POP
POP!
BEAST BOY?
I MUST HAVE FALLEN ASLEEP DURING MY BUTTERFLY HOMEWORK
WELL, THAT'S ONE WAY TO GET LOST IN A BOOK!
READIN'.

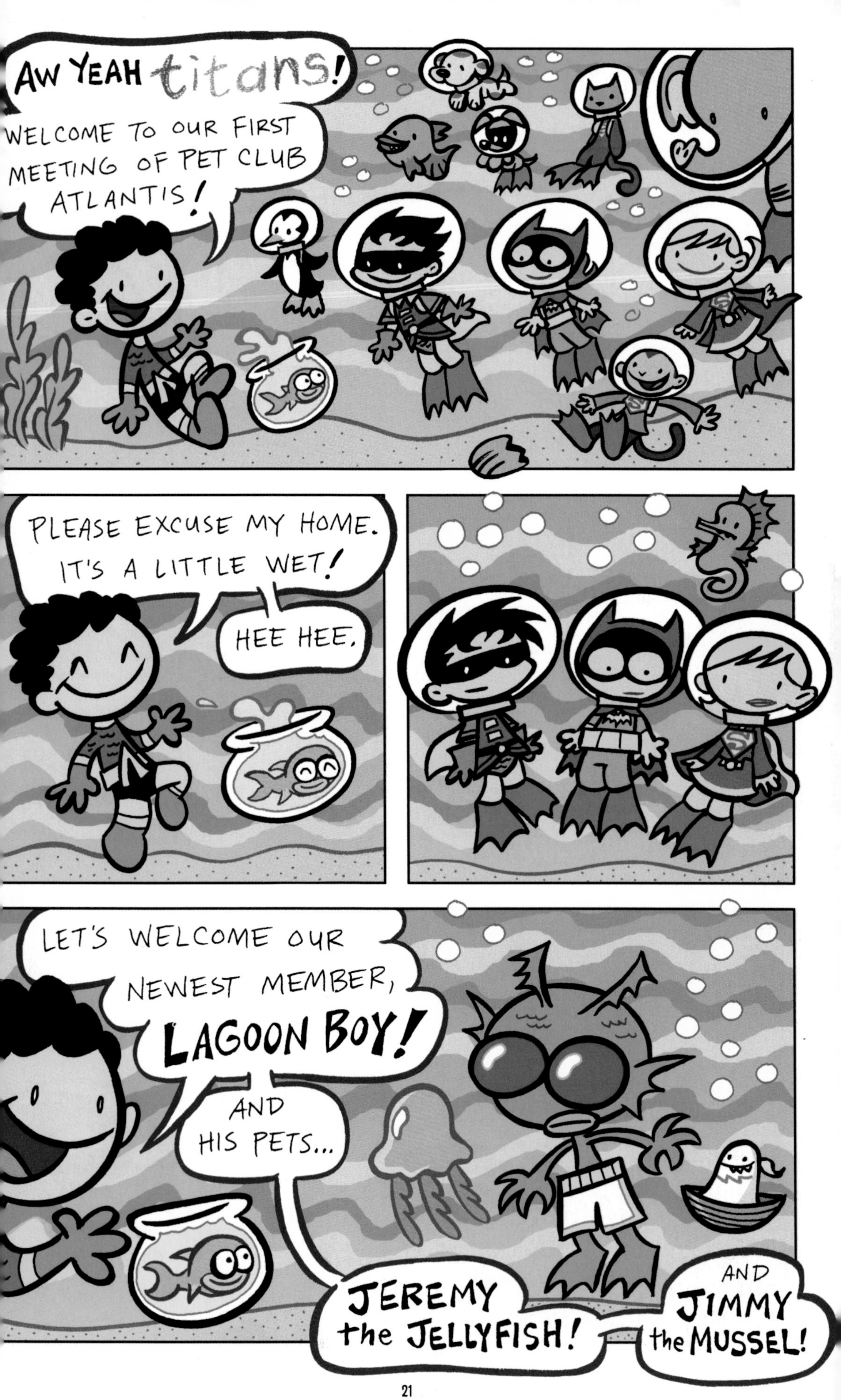
AW YEAH titans!
WELCOME TO OUR FIRST MEETING OF PET CLUB ATLANTIS!
PLEASE EXCUSE MY HOME. IT'S A LITTLE WET!
HEE HEE.
LET'S WELCOME OUR NEWEST MEMBER, LAGOON BOY!
AND HIS PETS...
JEREMY the JELLYFISH!
AND JIMMY the MUSSEL!

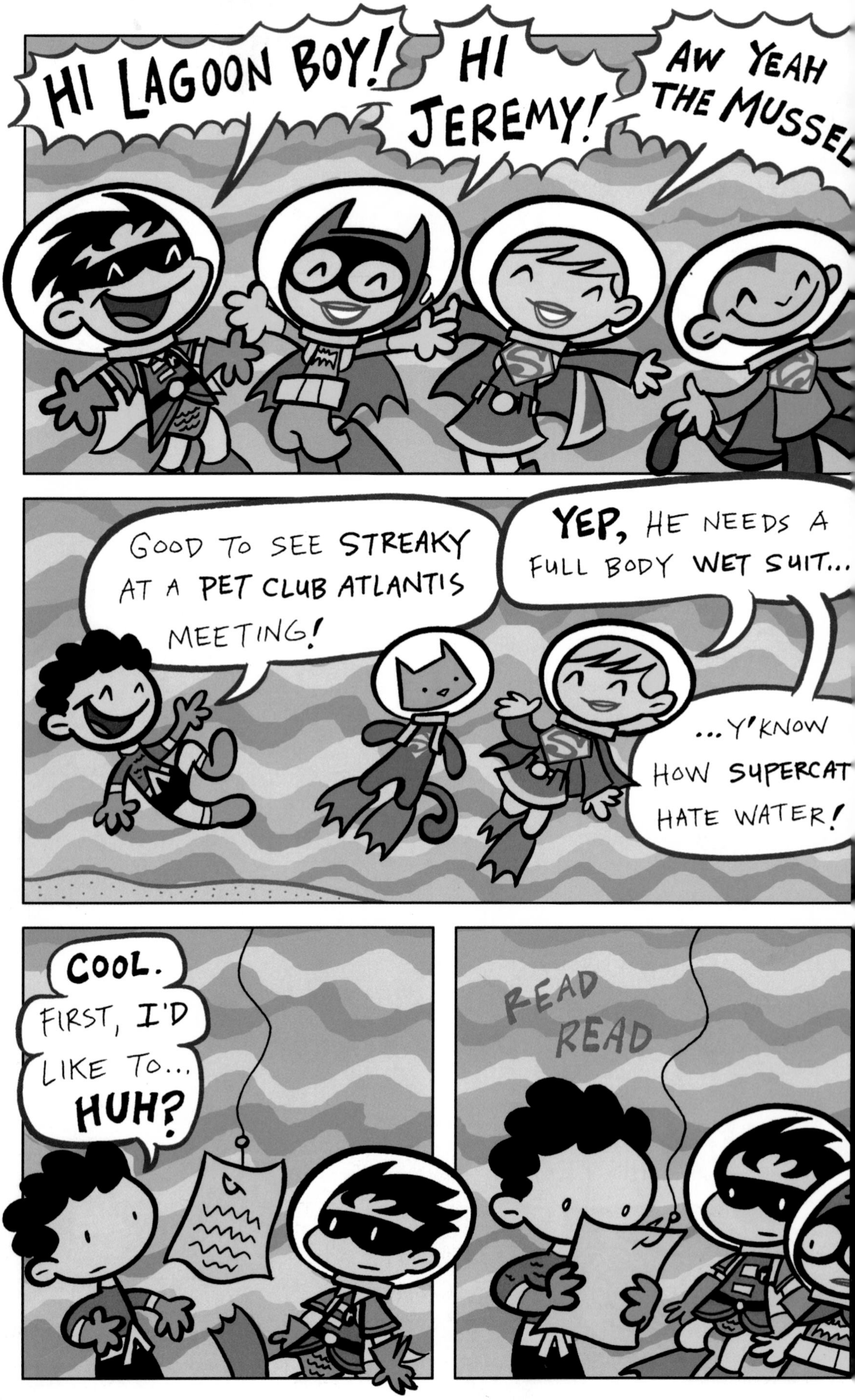
HI LAGOON BOY!
HI JEREMY!
AW YEAH THE MUSSEL
GOOD TO SEE STREAKY AT A PET CLUB ATLANTIS MEETING!
YEP, HE NEEDS A FULL BODY WET SUIT...
...Y'KNOW HOW SUPERCAT HATE WATER!
COOL. FIRST, I'D LIKE TO... HUH?
READ READ

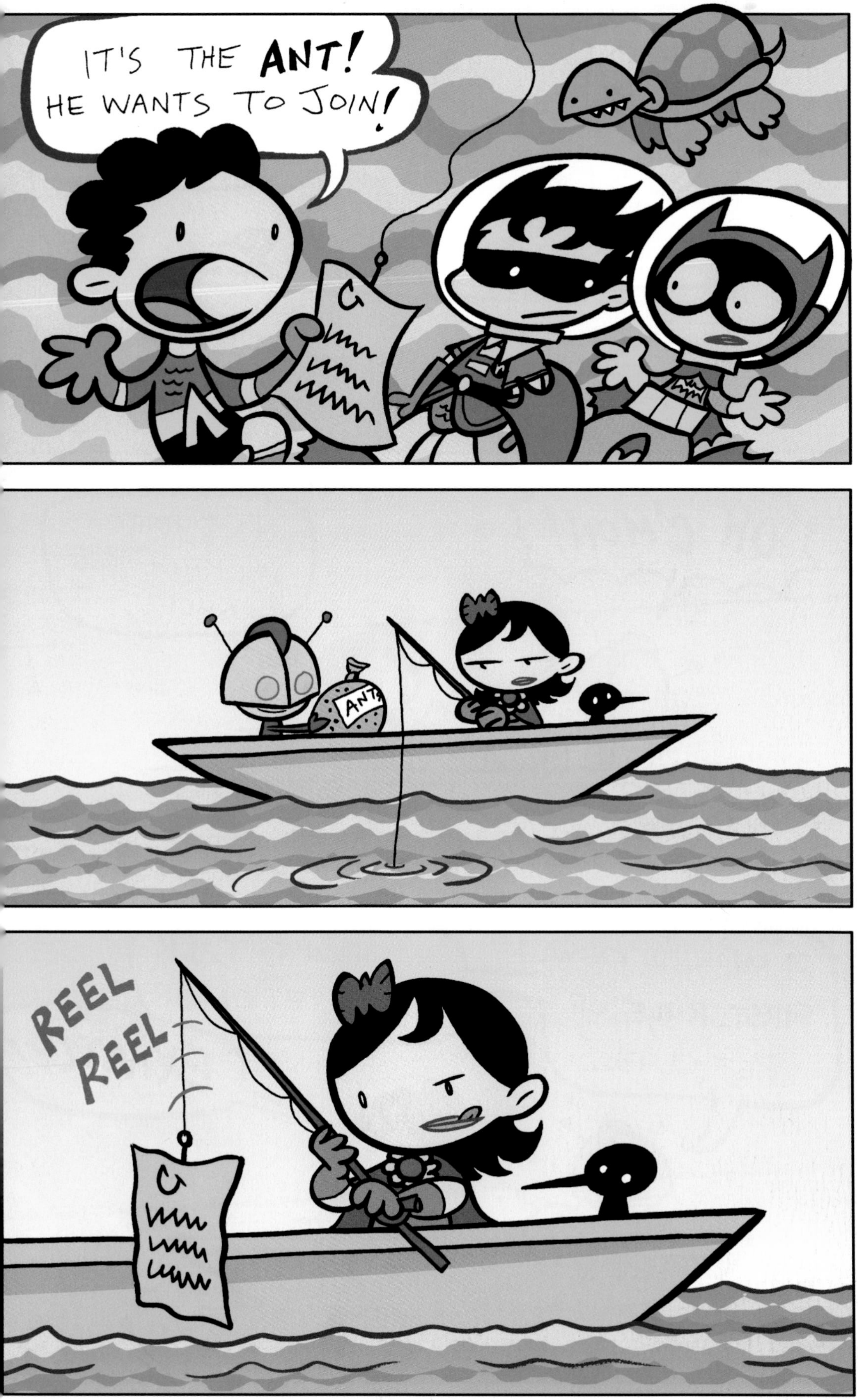
IT'S THE **ANT**! HE WANTS TO JOIN!
ANT
REEL
REEL

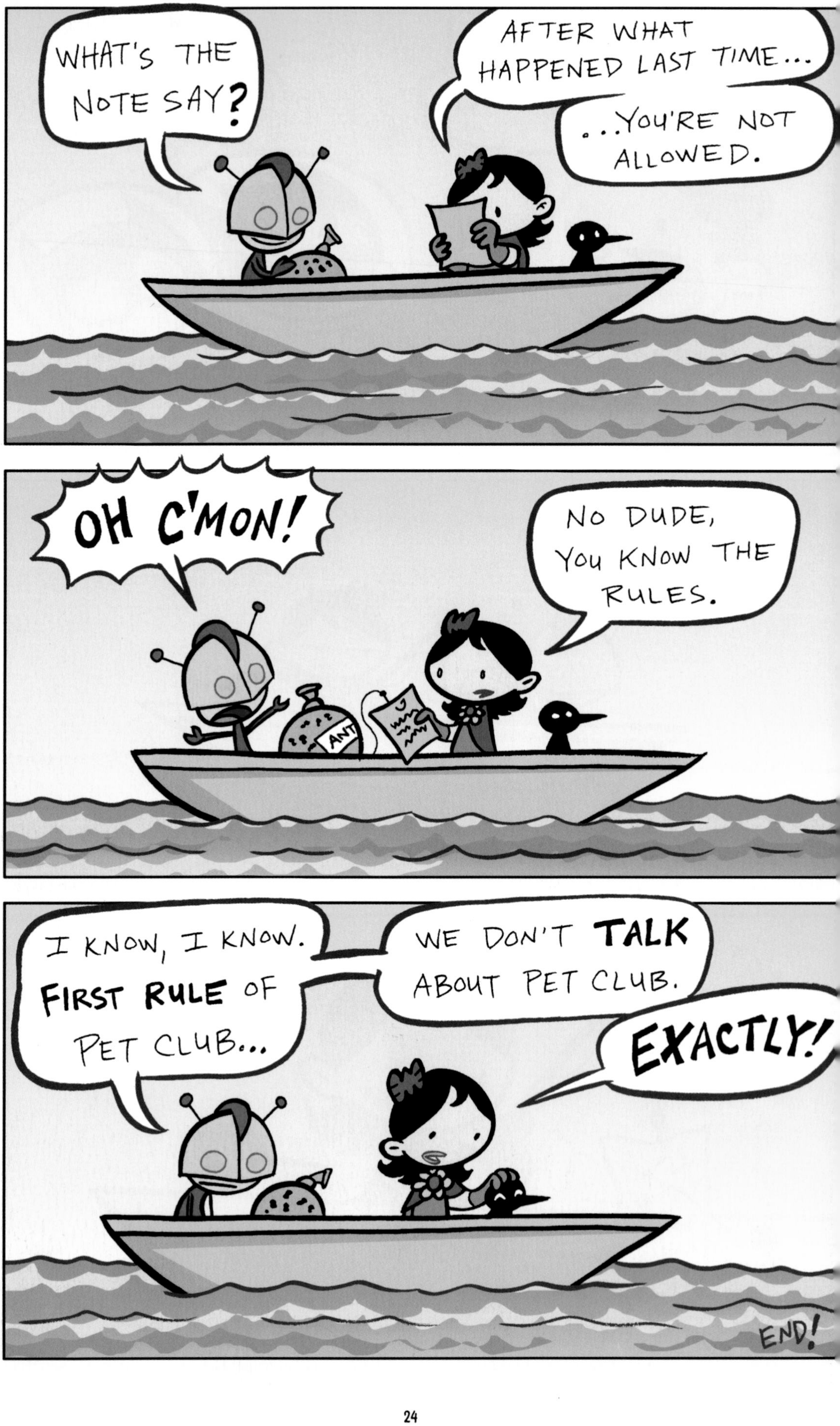
WHAT'S THE NOTE SAY?
AFTER WHAT HAPPENED LAST TIME...
...YOU'RE NOT ALLOWED.
OH C'MON!
NO DUDE, YOU KNOW THE RULES.
ANT
I KNOW, I KNOW. FIRST RULE OF PET CLUB...
WE DON'T TALK ABOUT PET CLUB.
EXACTLY!
END!

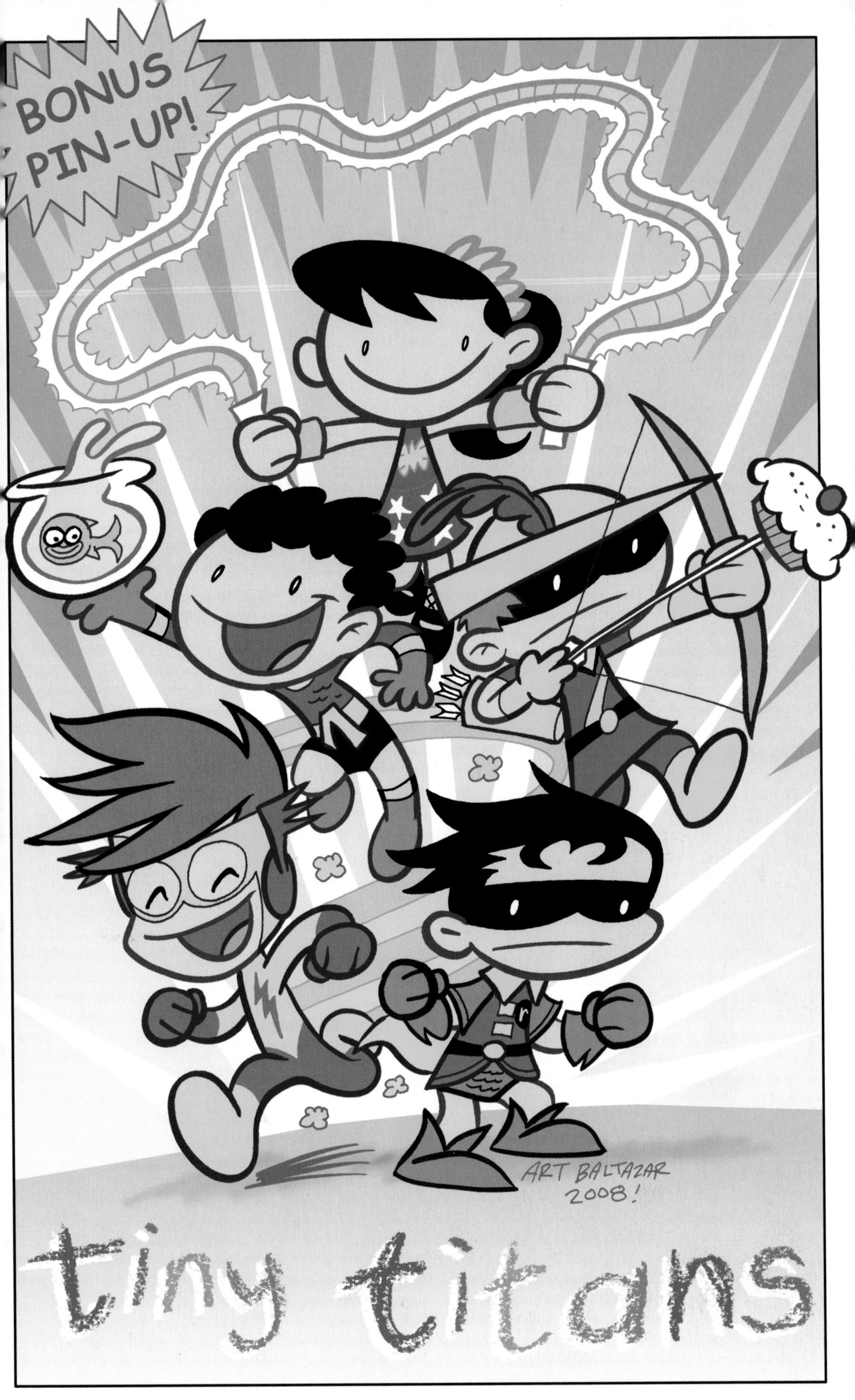
BONUS PIN-UP!
ART BALTAZAR 2008!
tiny titans

MEET THE... tiny titans

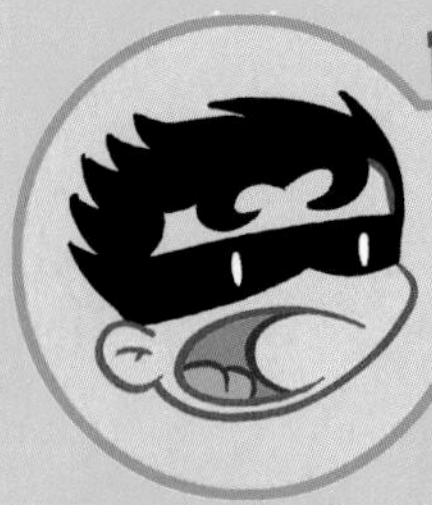

ROBIN

(Dick Grayson)- The brave and serious leader of the Tiny Titans. Although he is the original Robin, he is very moody and has to share his room with his brothers, the other Robins. Also, he has secret crushes for Starfire and Barbara Gordon.

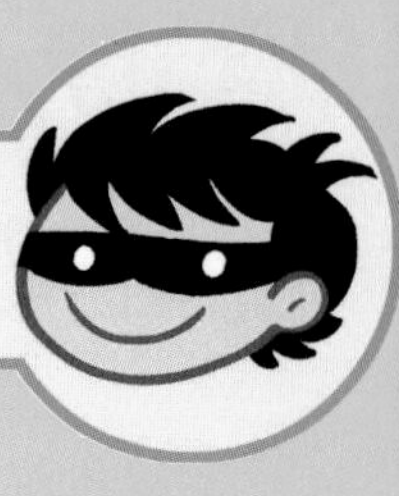

JASON TODDLER

The youngest of the three Robins. Too young to go to school, Jason is always in a happy mood and has a care-free style. He's all about smiling and having fun.

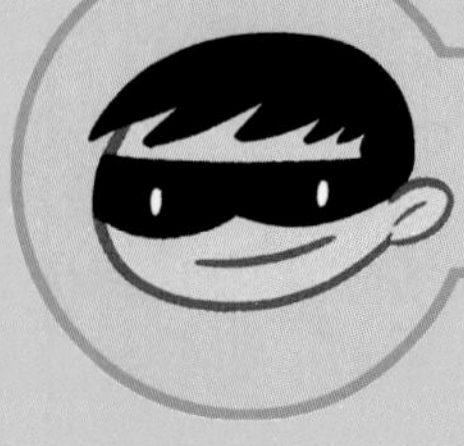

TIM DRAKE

The cool Robin. Tim wants to stand out from his brothers by wearing his own unique Robin costume. He's very laid back and easy going indeed.

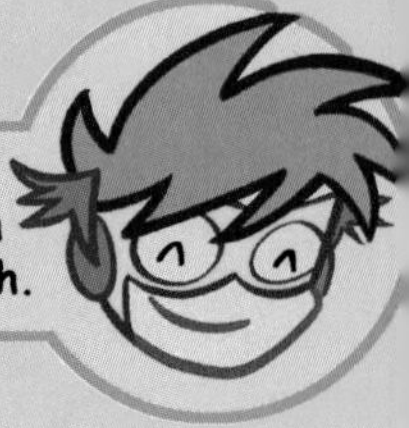

KID FLASH

The super speedster and fasted kid in the school. Quick witted and eats lots for lunch because of his high metabolism. Too much candy will cause major sugar rush.

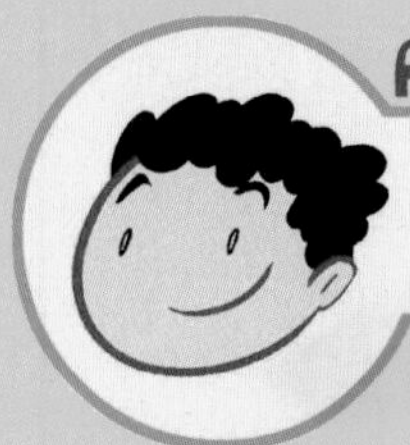

AQUALAD

The little boy from the ocean. Has a pet fish named Fluffy. Aqualad can communicate with all forms of sea life, even the pet hamster in their classroom.

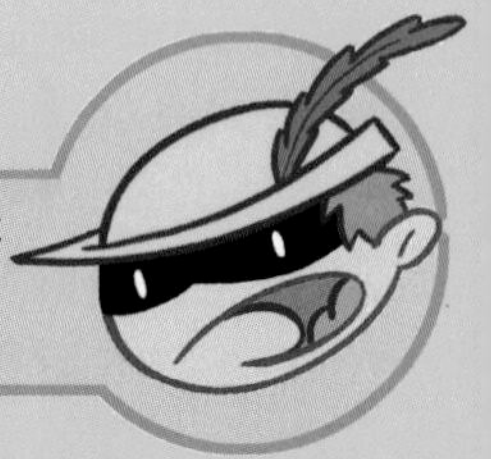

SPEEDY

Quiet and cool, he is the boy with the trick arrows. He's good at anything that requires aiming. Also, he's Kid Flash's best friend.

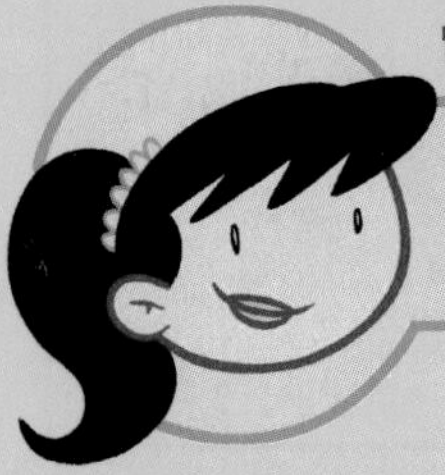

WONDER GIRL

(Donna) Raised by amazons. She's strong and cute. Never lie to her, she has a magical jump rope which makes people tell the truth. Very skeptic.

RAVEN

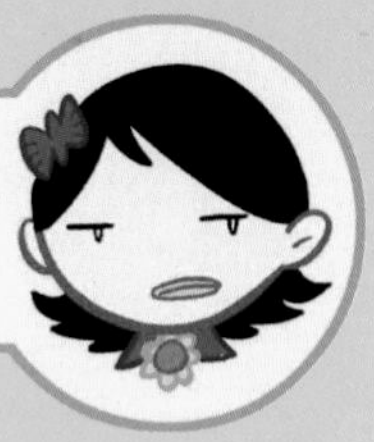

The quiet and mysterious little girl. She really likes to experiment with dark magic, which usually turn into bad practical jokes. Mr. Trigon, the substitute teacher is her father.

CYBORG

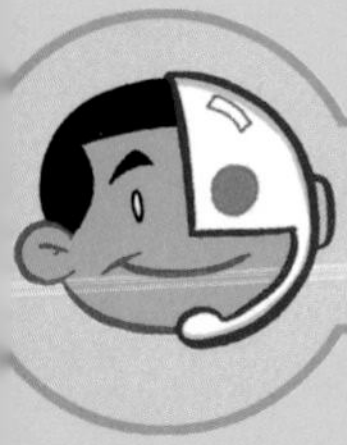

Half boy, half robot. Cyborg is always tinkering with mechanical gadgets, often turning them into something else. His battle cry "BOO-YA!" has earned him the nickname, "Big Boo-Ya".

BEAST BOY

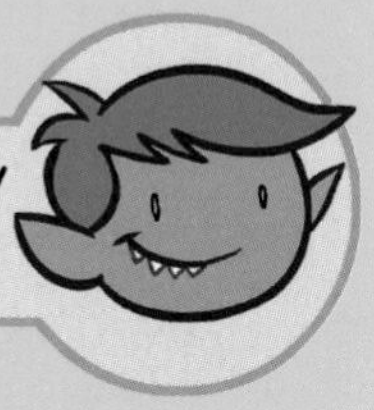

The green little boy who can change into any animal he desires. He's a prankster and loves comics. Has a crush on Terra.

STARFIRE

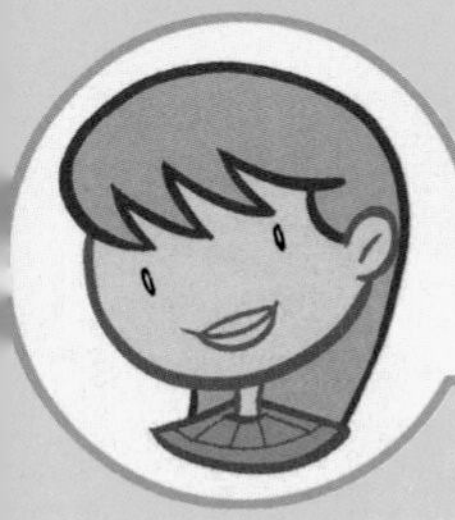

She's an alien princess. Very naïve and free spirited and finds the good in others. Has a crush on Robin and thinks he's cute, but so do all the other girls.

KID DEVIL

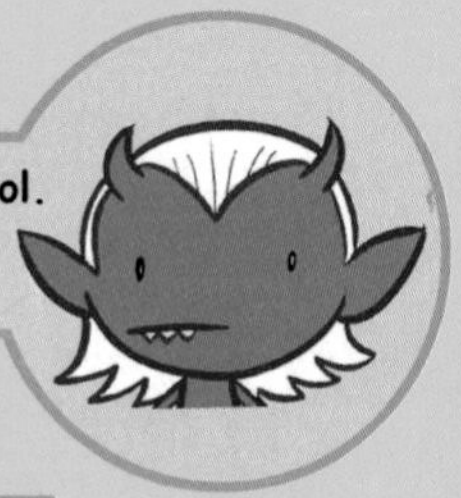

One of the younger Tiny Titans, still too young for school. Cannot talk but can breathe fire, usually while coughing or sneezing or hiccupping.

ROSE & JERICHO

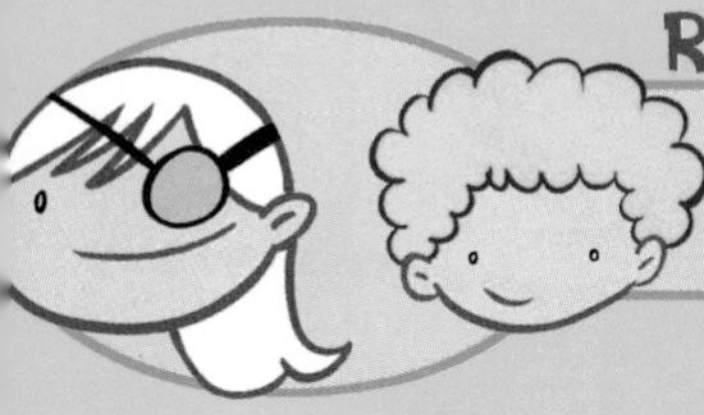

Principal Slade's kids. Rose is the older and tougher "Tom-Boy" of the two. Jericho can't speak, but can take over your mind if you look into his eyes.

MISS MARTIAN

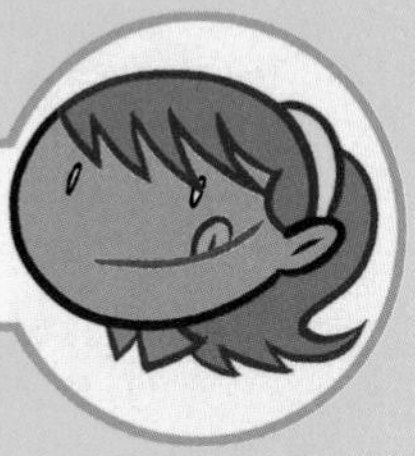

A shape shifting little girl alien from Mars who is still too young to go to school. She is often mistaken for Beast Boy's little sister.

TERRA

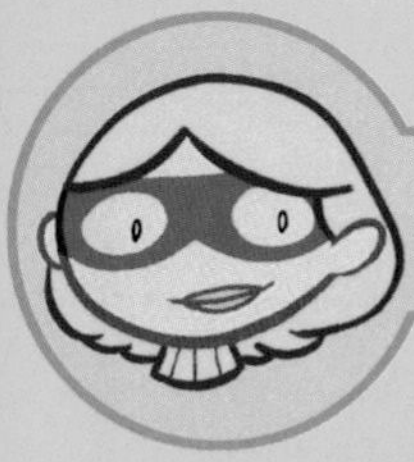

The sometimes hated little girl who likes to throw rocks. Principal Slade's teacher's pet. She thinks Beast Boy is a weirdo.

CASSIE

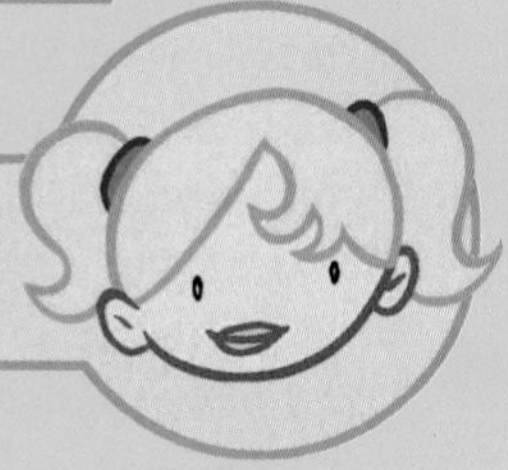

Wonder Girl's rich cousin from the big city. Cassie's really into fashion and is hip to all the latest trends in POP culture.

BUMBLE BEE

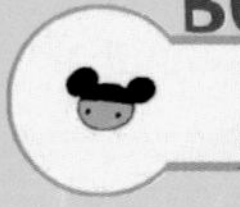

The tiniest of the Tiny Titans. BB buzzes and packs a mighty stinger.

Creators

Art Baltazar is a cartoonist machine from the heart of Chicago! He defines cartoons and comics not only as an art style, but as a way of life. Currently, Art is the creative force behind *The New York Times* best-selling, Eisner Award-winning, DC Comics series Tiny Titans, and the co-writer for Billy Batson and the Magic of SHAZAM! and co-creator of Superman Family Adventures. Art is living the dream! He draws comics and never has to leave the house. He lives with his lovely wife, Rose, big boy Sonny, little boy Gordon, and little girl Audrey. Right on!

ART BALTAZAR

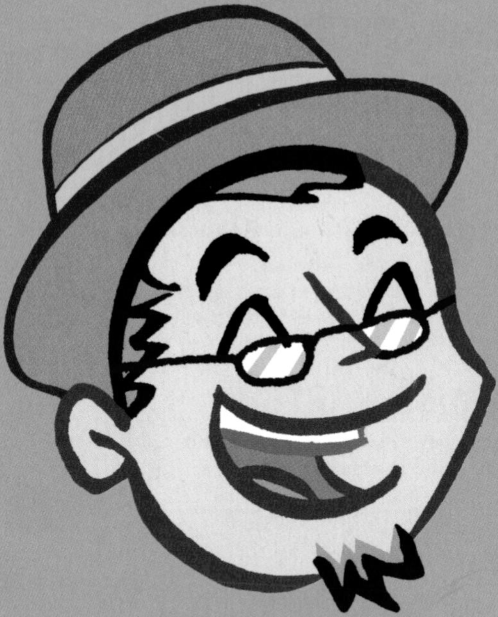

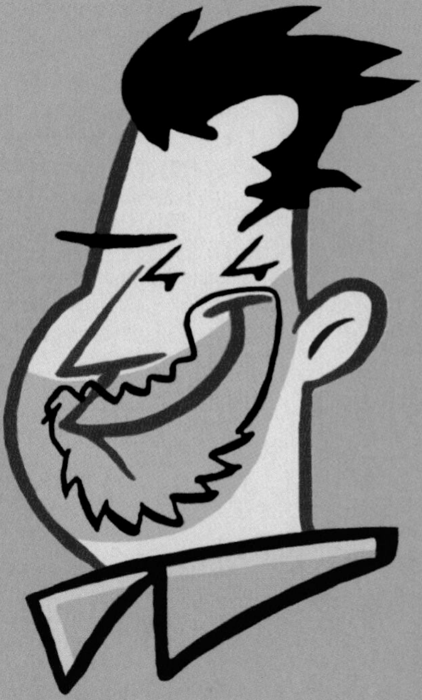

FRANCO

Bronx, New York born writer and artist Franco Aureliani has been drawing comics since he could hold a crayon. Currently residing in upstate New York with his wife, Ivette, and son, Nicolas, Franco spends most of his days in a Batcave-like studio where he produces DC's Tiny Titans comics. In 1995, Franco founded Blindwolf Studios, an independent art studio where he and fellow creators can create children's comics. Franco is the creator, artist, and writer of Weirdsville, L'il Creeps, and Eagle All Star, as well as the co-creator and writer of Patrick the Wolf Boy. When he's not writing and drawing, Franco also teaches high school art.

Glossary

ATTENTION [uh·TEN·shuhn] - careful listening or watching

CLICHÉ [klee·SHAY] - an idea or phrase that is used so often that it no longer has very much meaning

ENIGMA [i·NIG·muh] - a mystery or a puzzle

EXCEL [ek·SEL] - to do something extremely well

INVISIBLE [in·VIZ·uh·buhl] - something that cannot be seen

KNOWLEDGE [NOL·ij] - the things that someone knows

Action Accessories

Speedy

BOW AND ARROW

Robin

CAPE

Terra

ROCKS

Aqualad

FLUFFY

Wonder Girl

MAGIC JUMP ROPE

Visual Questions & Prompts

1. WHAT DO THINK BLUE BEETLE'S BACKPACK SAID TO HIM IN THE PANEL BELOW? WHAT CLUES DOES THE ILLUSTRATION OFFER?

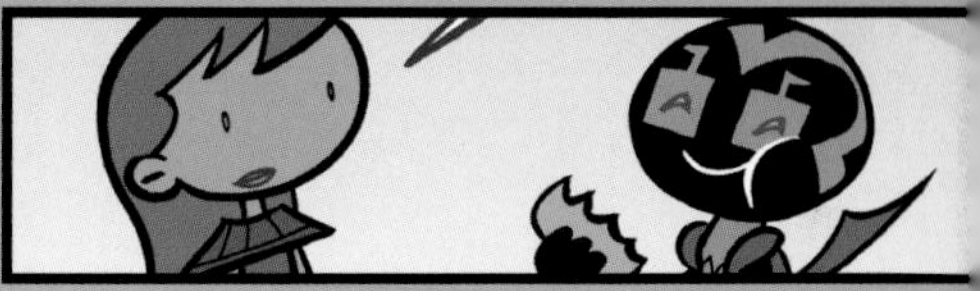

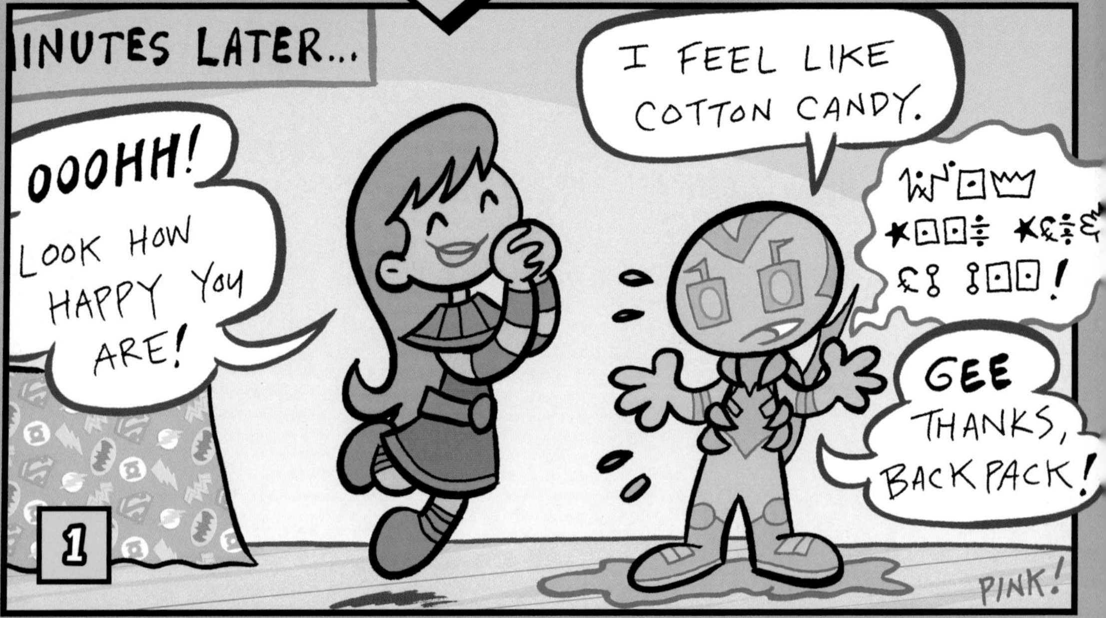
INUTES LATER...
OOOHH! LOOK HOW HAPPY YOU ARE!
I FEEL LIKE COTTON CANDY.
GEE THANKS, BACKPACK!
PINK!
1

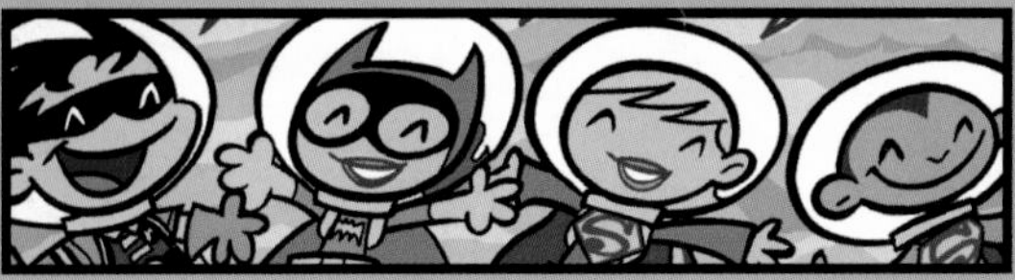

2. HOW CAN YOU TELL WHERE THE TINY TITANS ARE HOLDING THEIR PET CLUB MEETING? WHAT CLUES ARE THERE?

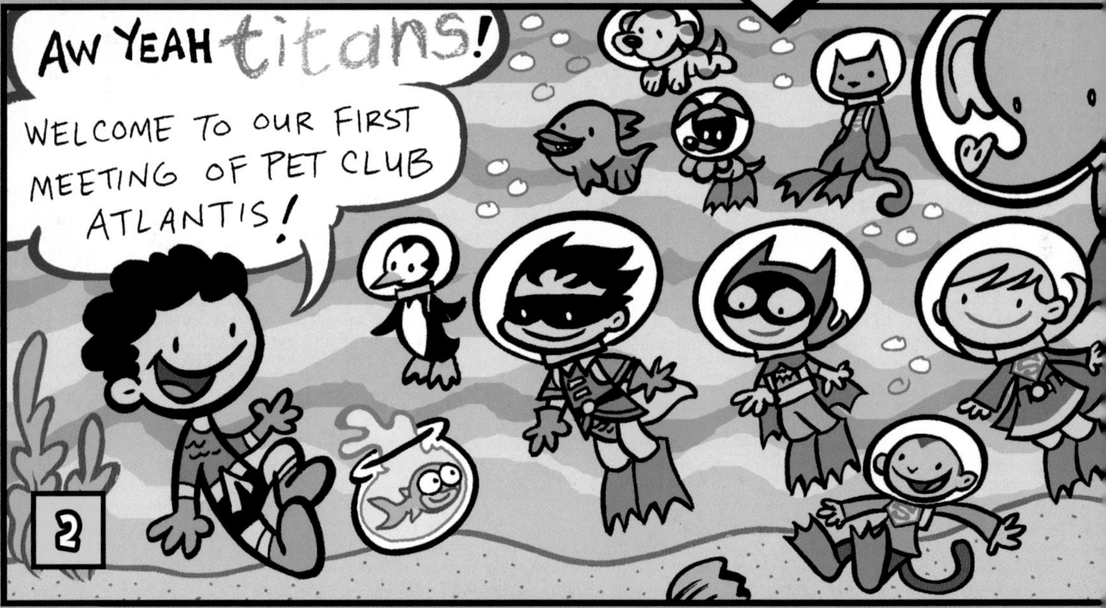
AW YEAH titans!
WELCOME TO OUR FIRST MEETING OF PET CLUB ATLANTIS!
2

3. SOMETIMES YOU DON'T NEED WORDS IN ORDER TO TELL A STORY. WRITE 2–3 SENTENCES EXPLAINING THE STORY IN THE PANELS BELOW.

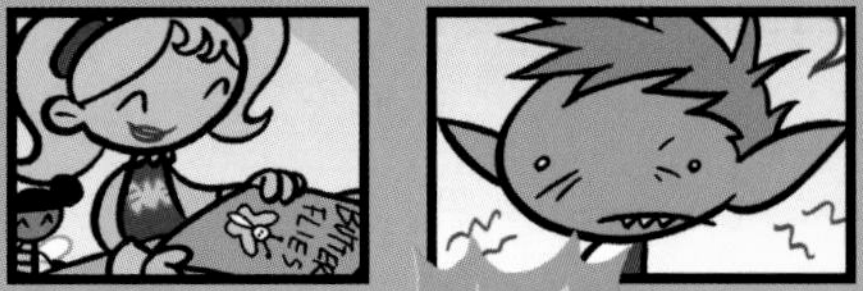

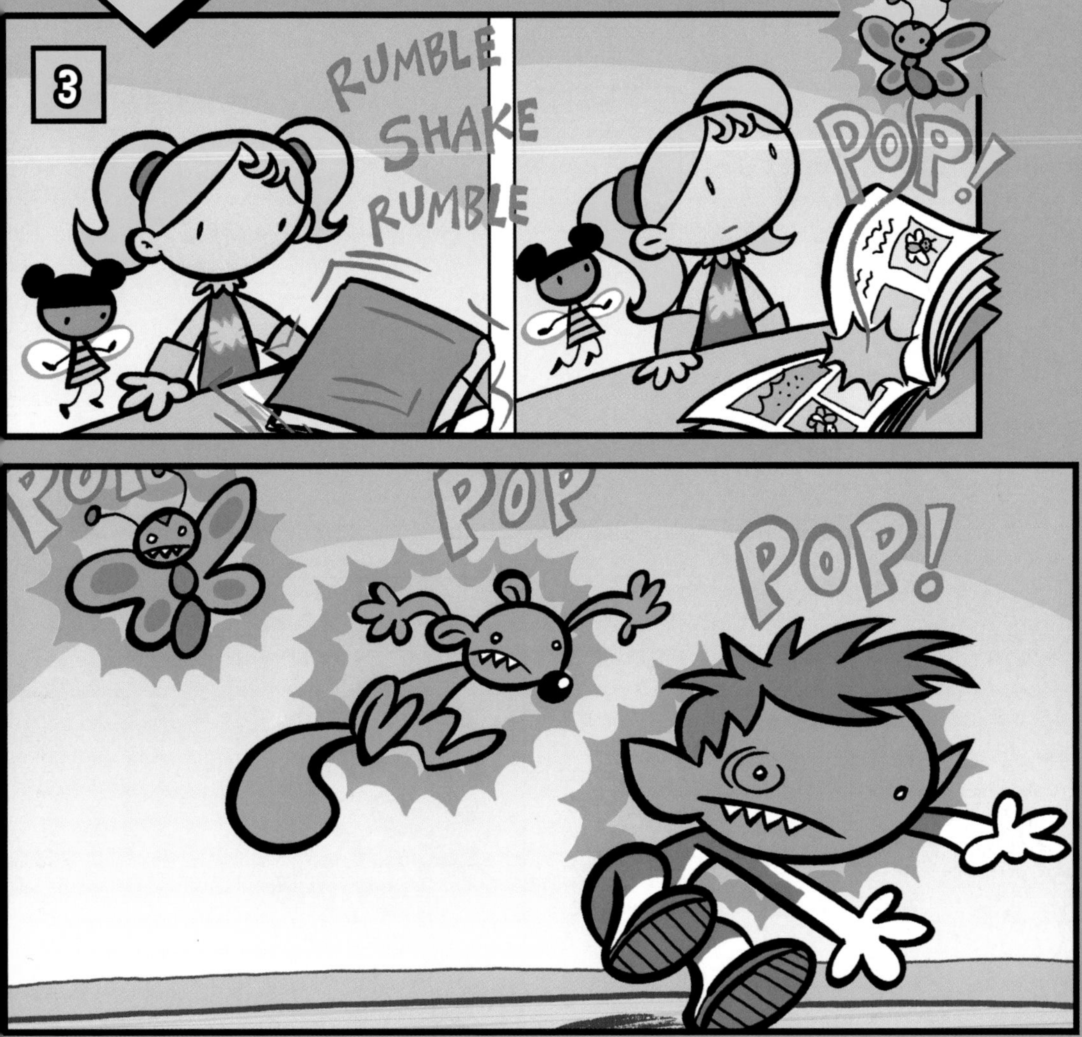
3
RUMBLE
SHAKE
RUMBLE
POP!
POP
POP!

4. WHAT DO YOU THINK HAPPENED LAST TIME ANT WENT TO PET CLUB THAT HE'S NOT ALLOWED BACK? USE YOUR IMAGINATION TO GUESS WHY.

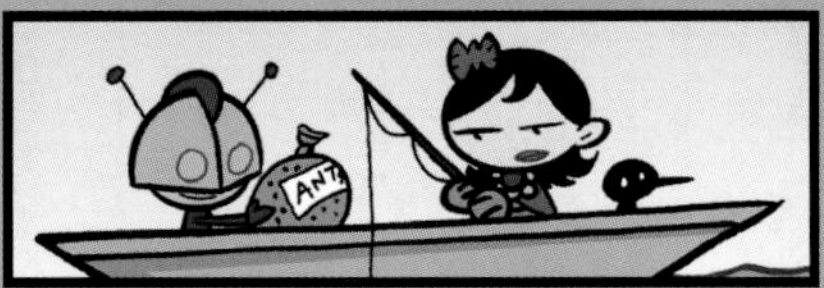

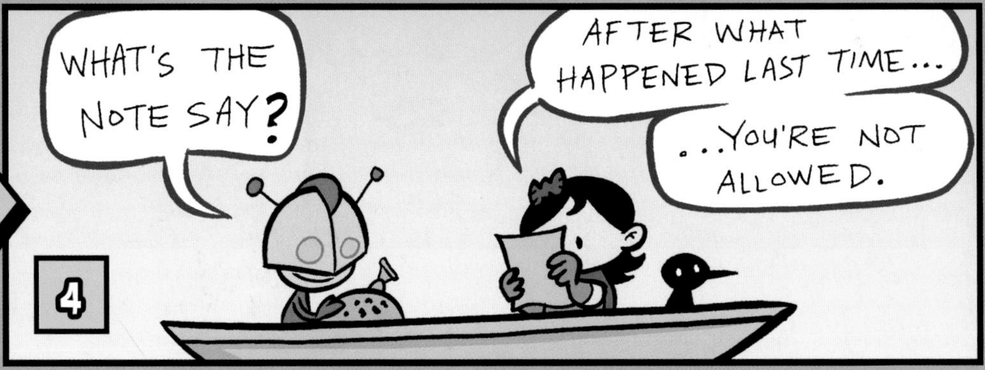
WHAT'S THE NOTE SAY?
AFTER WHAT HAPPENED LAST TIME...
...YOU'RE NOT ALLOWED.
4

tiny titans

tiny titans
Meet Tiny Titans East!
By Eisner Winners Art Baltazar & Franco
WHAT'S GOING ON?
I'M NOT SURE. IS IT ROBIN OR NIGHTWING?

tiny titans
Welcome to the Treehouse
AW YEAH, TITANS!
titans
AW YEAH, TITANS!
By Eisner Winners Art Baltazar & Franco

tiny titans
AAAHH!
DUDE, RELAX. IN SPACE, NO ONE CAN HEAR YOU SCREAM.
THAT'S FUNNY, IT'S PRETTY LOUD IN THIS COCKPIT!
By Eisner Winners Art Baltazar & Franco
Titans in Space

tiny titans
SIDEKICK CITY ELEMENTARY
AW YEAH, TITANS! WHAT GRADE DID YOU GET IN MATH?
I GOT AN "A"!
I GOT A "C".
I GOT A ROCK.
By Eisner Winners Art Baltazar & Franco
Report Card Pickup!

tiny titans
By Eisner Winners Art Baltazar & Franco
Sidekick City Elementary

tiny titans
vs. the Fearsome Five
By Eisner Winners Art Baltazar & Franco

tiny titans
AND I THOUGHT THE BATS WERE A PROBLEM!
By Eisner Winners Art Baltazar & Franco
Penguins in the Batcave!

tiny titans
Enter: Nightwing!
ROBIN, YOUR NEW COSTUME'S AWESOME!
AW YEAH! THIS DANCE PARTY ROCKS!
By Eisner Winners Art Baltazar & Franco

FIND COOL WEBSITES AND MORE BOOKS LIKE THIS ONE AT WWW.FACTHOUND.COM.
JUST TYPE IN THE BOOK ID: 978-1-4342-4699-8

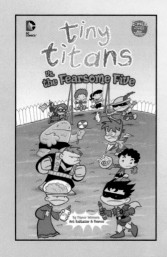